I0584240

VENGEANCE

VENGEANCE

ENEMY OF MY ENEMY™ BOOK FOUR

TIM MARQUITZ   MICHAEL ANDERLE
CRAIG MARTELLE

DISRUPTIVE IMAGINATION®

Vengeance (this book) is a work of fiction.

All of the characters, organizations, and events portrayed in this novel are either products of the author's imagination or are used fictitiously. Sometimes both.

Copyright © 2019 Tim Marquitz, Michael Anderle and Craig Martelle
Cover by Tom Edwards tomedwardsdesign.com/
Cover copyright © LMBPN Publishing
A Michael Anderle Production

LMBPN Publishing supports the right to free expression and the value of copyright. The purpose of copyright is to encourage writers and artists to produce the creative works that enrich our culture.

The distribution of this book without permission is a theft of the author's intellectual property. If you would like permission to use material from the book (other than for review purposes), please contact support@lmbpn.com. Thank you for your support of the author's rights.

LMBPN Publishing
PMB 196, 2540 South Maryland Pkwy
Las Vegas, NV 89109

First US edition, January 2019

The Kurtherian Gambit (and what happens within / characters / situations / worlds) are copyright © 2015-2019 by Michael T. Anderle and LMBPN Publishing.

VENGEANCE TEAM

Thanks to the JIT Readers

Diane L. Smith
Jeff Eaton
James Caplan
Micky Cocker
Kelly O'Donnell
Peter Manis

If I've missed anyone, please let me know!

Editor
Skyhunter Editing Team

CHAPTER ONE

Planning a war is hard.

Taj stared at the myriad waves of information filling the view screen for about the millionth time today, not even counting all the other times she'd gone over it recently.

There was no putting it off any longer. The time had come.

"I think we're ready," she announced.

"Finally. It's only taken about three months," Torbon complained.

"Everything has to be perfect. Well, as perfect as we can make it with what we've got available to us." she countered, sneering at Torbon and waggling a fist his direction.

His whiskers flared and he raised his hands in surrender, his tail thumping against the chair leg. "Yeah, definitely looks like you're ready for a fight, but how about you save it for the enemy, huh?"

Lina slapped Torbon on the arm to shut him up, but Taj

could tell the engineer agreed with Torbon. Her expression said it all.

Everyone was impatient, but they were doing this largely on their own—which was the way Taj and her people had wanted it.

When Lance Reynolds had offered them the full support of the Federation's military but warned it could take another year before that could be put in place because of ongoing operations and longer if more pressing matters came up, Taj had thanked him and passed.

Politely, of course.

They wanted their home back now.

Reynolds had argued against them going off on their own, joking that it was like herding cats to get Taj to see reason, but there was more to this for the Furlorians than simply reclaiming their planet.

As a point of pride, they needed to do it themselves.

They didn't want anyone else fighting their war for them. This was on them; their mission, and Taj had assured Reynolds she understood when he said they would be entirely on their own if they chose to go at it this way.

Reynolds had provided what he could in the limited time available.

"So, when do we go?" Lina asked, interrupting Taj's thoughts.

Taj drew in a long, deep breath and let it out slowly. "Now is as good a time as any, I guess," she answered. "The longer we wait, the more time the Wyyvans have to settle in, do damage to the planet, and make it harder to get back."

Her thoughts drifted to Krawlas, the Furlorian home

world that she and the crew had abandoned almost exactly one year before.

It seemed like much longer than that.

They'd lost so many people. Gran Beaux and Mama Merr most notably, but that only scratched the surface of the harm that had been wrought upon the Furlorians since the lizard-like Wyyvans had crash-landed on the planet out of nowhere and uprooted their existence.

It was strange looking back on it now. Things were so different.

It'd been traumatic early on. Their lives thrown into chaos, the fight against the Wyyvan troops, then the fleet's assault on the planet, followed by their flight into space with no clear direction or idea as to what they were going to do.

Finding Dent had been the start of their orientation, she realized, remembering rescuing him from his wrecked science ship in the old android body the AI had inhabited. He'd been the one to turn the Furlorians around since he'd helped them connect with the Etheric Federation.

Taj and the crew had grown up a lot since then that it seemed unreal to her, but there was still so much more to accomplish.

Like now. Here she was, in charge of a ramshackle armada of spacecraft, hobbled together out of old, decommissioned ships that could be rounded up quickly, readying to return to Krawlas and take it back from the Wyyvans.

Cabe ran a warm hand over the back of her neck, clasping her shoulder. "You okay?" he asked. "You seem a bit...pensive."

She offered him a weak smile. "This is a big decision to commit us to," she explained. "I'm worried, that's all."

It wasn't that she was unsure. No, quite the opposite, in fact.

She was surer than ever that this was the right thing to do: to take the fight to the alien scum who had stolen their home world. Taj couldn't imagine anything that felt more justified than swooping in over Krawlas and kicking the asses of each and every Wyyvan there who had dared to spoil their home.

Her only real concern was the danger she was putting her crew in. It was one thing to make a decision that affected only her and dive into a battle alone, but it was something entirely different to drag people along with her; people who might die because of her leadership.

"Of course it is," he replied as if reading her mind. It was something he'd started to do more often as the couple became closer. "But this isn't just on you. We *all* decided this was the right thing to do, remember?"

Sure they had, she thought, but was it because she had pushed for it? Because she had wanted it so badly?

She'd argued with herself for a long time after asking General Reynolds for a force to take back Krawlas. She hadn't consulted them beforehand and had simply acted on a whim, believing it was what needed to be done. But had she made the right choice by dragging everyone into the fight with her?

Cabe squeezed her shoulder again, reassuring her that she had and that this what they had *all* wanted.

"We're all a part of this, and nothing is going to stop us

from taking our home back from those gacking aliens," Cabe exclaimed. "Nothing."

Lina grinned her agreement, nodding.

"Except dying," Torbon added, "or capture. Or maybe scurvy or some other nasty disease I haven't thought of." He shrugged.

Everyone glared at him, and he shriveled into his chair under the pressure.

"But yeah, nothing's gonna stop us," he amended. "Rowl be damned."

Taj groaned and clambered to her feet.

"You just had to go and invoke Rowl, didn't you?" Cabe flicked Torbon's ear, causing him to hiss and duck away.

Lina flicked the other one as he leaned her way. Torbon growled and covered his head, trying to protect himself from each side.

"You deserved both of those," the engineer informed him, shaking her head as she stood.

"Let's go get Dent and the others and get this war on the road," Taj stated, taking one last look at the planning room they'd commandeered on the Corzant space station.

It was hard for her to imagine that they would likely never see this room, or possibly even the station, again.

That was a sobering thought Taj didn't appreciate, so she swept it from her mind and promised herself that, no matter what happened, she and the crew would come back and visit once everything was settled.

Since they were leaving the vast majority of their people behind for safekeeping rather than dragging them into battle, they had a good reason to come back, even if it was only to collect the Furlorians and escort them home.

She grinned at that thought and marched toward the shuttle that would take them to the Furlorian command ship.

Today was a monumental day, and Taj would be gacked if she let her uncertainty get in the way.

Her crew didn't even bother to ask if she was sure, which they always did regardless of how much she hated that gacking question. They could see the determination in her eyes.

At long last, they were going home.

The Gate eased open before the Furlorian armada, and a rush of excitement set the blood afire in Taj's veins.

The time was now. They were truly doing this.

She glanced at the view screen and examined the fleet of ships stacked up behind the lead craft. It was a sight to behold.

Born and raised on the scrubland planet of Krawlas, she'd grown up imagining a day where she would lead an army into battle. Gran Beaux had trained her to lead and put his faith in her, but she'd never imagined she'd get the opportunity to do so. Life on Krawlas had always been peaceful, its remoteness the main reason the Furlorians had settled there after being driven from their ancestral home world, Felinus 4.

All that had changed when the Wyyvans arrived, though, and here she was at the helm of a destroyer, ready to charge through an intergalactic Gate and engage the enemy just a short distance away on the other side.

"The Gate's fully open," Dent called from beside her. "Waiting on your order," he added, offering her a respectful nod.

Taj stood still, taking the moment in and savoring the calm before the storm that would engulf them once they passed through the shimmering Gate. The minute she ordered them forward, there was no retreat. They were committed.

Fortunately, she'd decided early on that she wouldn't put any more of her people at risk than she absolutely had to. With barely more than thirty Furlorians aboard the *Decimator*, Taj's name for the destroyer she and her people would ride into the fight, she knew her people would live on, regardless of the outcome.

The remainder of the ships were manned by a large contingent of bots for damage repair and various menial tasks, but it was Dent who controlled the entire fleet.

He had linked himself to all the crafts to minimize the number of lives put at risk, as Taj had requested once their plans began to come together.

In the end, Taj was glad it had worked out that way, but that hadn't been what she'd envisioned when she'd first asked the General for an army.

She'd originally pictured a storm of trained and experienced Federation soldiers in powered armor riding down on the Wyyvans and crushing them like gralflies under a swatter.

But where was the satisfaction in that?

In the end, to feel good about what they'd accomplished and to honor those who'd come before, the victory had to be on their terms.

She and her crew would reach out to Reynolds as soon as they reclaimed Krawlas, and they would make the Federation proud.

General Reynolds had grinned and graciously said, "Damn right, you will. Now go kick lizard tail, and bring me back a pair of boots when you're done."

With Reynolds' words ringing in her head, Taj grinned and waved the armada toward the yawning Gate.

"Let's do this," she ordered, taking one last look at the crew gathered around her.

Cabe stood at her side next to Dent, and Lina and Torbon were right there, too. Jadie, Torbon's aunt, grinned, ready to go, and Kal stood proudly in his armor, happy for the chance to wreak vengeance on the Wyyvans.

Krawg sat at a console in the background watching over everything, as he often did. Taj had given him a chance to return home, but he'd refused. For all his grumpiness, it was clear he liked the Furlorians. Even more, he enjoyed the excitement that came with being around them.

He'd deny it if he were asked, of course, but Taj knew better.

Plus, he liked arguing with Torbon. Some days, it seemed as if that was all they did.

The fleet shot forward at her command, and Taj's heart thundered in her chest with anticipation.

She'd long dreamed of this moment, studied and planned, and here it was at last.

The Furlorian fleet shot through the Gate, shields and weapons powered up and at the ready—a tip provided her by General Reynolds, ensuring that she and her people were ready for whatever they met on the other side of the Gate.

As the Gate closed behind them, Taj caught her breath and oriented herself.

Krawlas sat in space nearby, filling the view screen with its presence. Her crew gasped behind her, amazed by the sight.

None of them had seen the planet since they'd fled it, and their return filled each of them with a joy they hadn't realized they were capable of.

Unfortunately, the realization that an enemy fleet sat in orbit above the planet twisted that feeling and turned it to righteous anger. The bridge lights dimmed and became red, an ominous gleam washing over the crew as if it had sensed their moods.

"Enemy fleet dead ahead," Lina announced, her voice hard and cold. "Looks like they have twenty-five destroyers out here now, not to mention the command dreadnought that bombarded us when Vort's cohorts showed up the first time around."

Taj nodded, her eyes drawn to the looming dread-nought that had plagued her dreams more times in the last year than she would ever admit aloud.

Today, however, it didn't scare her.

Seeing the massive ship floating in orbit above her home world brought a rage to her belly that threatened to consume her. Her cheeks flared warmly, and she let out a low, rumbling growl. She knew what she needed to do.

Now wasn't the time to stare in awe and hesitate.

Now was the time to act.

"Blow that gacking piece of shit out of the sky," she

ordered, jabbing her finger at the dreadnought on the screen.

The Furlorian armada spread out at her command, Dent grinning all the while, and the ships opened fire without mercy or warning.

Just like they did to us, Taj thought, remembering the day the crew had gone to examine the wrecked ship that had crashed on Krawlas.

The Wyyvan fleet, caught unprepared, lost two ships in the initial volley before they reacted.

As those two destroyers flared out and listed, falling toward the planet below, the Wyyvans returned fire. The blackness of space was then illuminated by blasts from Wyyvan weapons, but the reinforced shields of the Furlorian armada held.

Taj whooped and urged the fleet forward. "Take the fight to them," she ordered, determined to make the most of their surprise arrival.

"They're hailing us," Lina announced. "Asking who we are and why we're attacking. Response?"

"Gack them!" Taj shot back, waving a hand to dismiss the communication. "Ignore it and keep blasting, focusing as much fire on that dreadnought as possible. I want to punch a hole in it."

With no living beings aboard any of the ships except the *Decimator,* Taj could act with confidence that she wasn't condemning anyone to a horrible death. That knowledge emboldened her.

It's easier to fight a war when people won't die for your mistakes, Taj thought, her hands clenching the edge of the console before her.

The *Decimator* hung back slightly, using the unmanned vessels for cover while the armada advanced as they'd planned, the fleet blasting at the enemy ships.

Wave after wave of energy assailed the Wyyvan fleet, and another of their ships broke apart and exploded. Debris and vented atmosphere flashed silver in the gleam of weapons fire, then vanished as if it had never existed.

Torbon whooped in the background, and although Taj wanted to join him, she needed to keep her focus. No matter how well they were doing, the fight was a long way from being over.

It had only just begun.

"Keep pressing," she called, her knuckles aching from how tight she'd been holding the console. "Don't let up. If we can put them down now, let's do it."

She understood that was unlikely, but it didn't stop her from trying.

Taj forced her hands to let go and dropped into the captain's seat behind her, feeling the tightness in her legs. She made herself relax, a herculean task, and drew in a deep breath to temper her excitement and counter the adrenaline raging through her.

She knew the rest of the crew were doing the same. They'd all wanted this so badly.

Fortunately, regardless of how excited or desperate the crew might be, Taj knew Dent would hold it together.

Being an AI, he had no emotional attachment that would affect the fight or its outcome. Still, he wanted the victory as much as they did, even if his reasoning was more logic-based and rationally determined.

Taj had promised Dent that he could resurrect his

people, the Dandrinites, on Krawlas, and they could live side by side with the Furlorians and make a new life for all of them. Their two peoples could start over together.

Dent had loved the idea, and he had given the mission his all from the start. His perseverance paid off.

"Look!" Kal cried out. "They're breaking already."

Taj watched as another Wyyvan destroyer exploded beside the command ship, reveling in seeing it fly into pieces that battered the shields of its companions with brilliant sparks that died as soon as they were born.

"The dreadnought is pulling back," Dent reported, confirming what Kal had seen, "and taking cover behind the other ships. Looks like we've wounded it, though not seriously."

"What are the chances we can end it now?" Taj asked, although she already knew the answer.

"Not likely," Dent replied, not bothering to pretend they had more of an opportunity than they did. "All we can do is keep hammering it and hope its captain continues to blink."

"We're still outnumbered," Cabe reported, "and we've just lost our first ship, but I don't think all that's sunk into their lizard brains yet. They just know they're being shot at."

"He's right," Dent replied. "Their fleet is moving into a defensive posture, adjusting to protect the dreadnought at the expense of the other ships. It looks as though they're retreating, looking to regroup. They weren't ready for us, and don't want to risk further losses, from what I can assess."

"That's a good thing, right?" Taj asked.

"Could be." Dent shrugged. "Depends on how you look at it," he explained. "Any reasonable commander would judge what's happened here as a temporary setback, nothing more. We surprised them, got in a good first punch, and bloodied their nose before they saw it coming, but they're going to step back and reassess, then come at us in a way that makes the most of their advantages."

"Which includes way more ships and a gacking metric ton of firepower," Lina announced.

"And they'll have eliminated our initial surprise," Dent finished.

Taj watched the Wyyvan fleet pulling back on the screen, her jaw clenched. It was a pleasure to watch the Wyyvan scum retreat, but she understood that this was hardly a victory to celebrate.

While the Furlorian armada continued to pound the Wyyvan ships, the lizards fought back. Another of the automated ships under Dent's control was damaged and began to list out of control. Dent let it go and Taj followed its spinning passage into space on her scanners, simply glad there was no one alive aboard it.

Although she understood its importance, in her mind, she couldn't help but picture the ship as a game piece that had been swept off the board. It carried no emotional resonance, and she wondered for a second if that was how Dent felt.

Once the ship had flared out, she turned her attention back to the retreating Wyyvan ships and growled at them.

They were something she could get worked up about.

For all her dreams of riding in and obliterating the enemy in a single decisive blow, she'd known that wasn't how it was going to go down. That hadn't stopped her from hoping, however.

But she wouldn't let that get in the way of the job she had come to do.

As the first engagement waned, the Wyyvans pulling away, Taj knew what she had to do.

"Scan the planet and pinpoint all those gackball lizards," she commanded. "I want to rain fire down on them like they did us not too long ago. Show them what it feels like."

A few seconds later, Lina groaned at her station. "Hate to say it, but it's not gonna be that easy," she told Taj.

"What do you mean?" Taj asked.

"The Wyyvans aren't alone on the planet," Lina reported.

"What?" Taj shouted, spinning around in her seat to glare at the engineer.

Dent came over to stand beside Lina. A sneer twisted his handsome face into something sinister as he confirmed her assessment.

"She's right," the AI proclaimed. "I'm picking up a wide range of non-Wyyvan lifeforms below. Hundreds of them, and a number of different species."

"Slave labor," Jadie said, her voice little more than a whisper. The words, however, pressed down upon the crew like a heavy blanket.

"Captain Vort was using his own people to dig for the Toradium-42," Taj mused, her mind whirling. "Why would he—"

"This isn't Vort we're dealing with," Cabe explained, shaking his shaggy head. His tail whipped back and forth with a menacing flick. "Vort was desperate to steal as much of the mineral as he could before his superiors arrived and realized it, remember? He was using his soldiers out of necessity and convenience."

"Which doesn't make sense in the long-term," Lina finished, gesturing to the console and her readings. "Why run your troops down when you can enslave people and make them do the work for you?"

"So, we can't just blow these gacks away from up here," Taj said, realization sinking in and forming a strangling knot in her guts. "Bloody Rowl!"

So much for everything being perfect.

What's that saying? "No plan survives the first engagement?"

"That's not our only problem," Dent told them, offering them more bad news. He brought an image up on the screen, focusing on an area of space behind the retreating Wyyvan fleet. "You see that?"

A metallic ring floated in the blackness, only the barest of lights on its surface defining it against the deeper darkness that surrounded it. It loomed ominously; it wasn't quite the size of the Corzant space station, but it was monstrous.

Two destroyers sat alongside it, giving context to its size.

"What the gack is that thing?" Torbon asked.

"A temporary Gate," the AI replied.

"Wait, you mean they have their own Gate?" Taj asked.

Dent nodded. "That's exactly the case."

"Which means they can supplement their already-superior force while we can't." Cabe groaned.

"We are so—" Torbon started, but Taj cut him off.

"You finish that statement, and I dump you with the

trash and push you at the Wyyvans," Taj warned with a growl. "We didn't come here to lose, and I'll be gacked if we're giving up this early into the fight, no matter *what* kind of toys the Wyyvans have to play with."

She jumped out of her seat and motioned for the crew to follow her as she started off the bridge.

"Looks like we'll have to take the fight to the planet before the enemy fleet wraps their head around getting their asses kicked and calls home for backup," she announced. "Any way to block their communications while we do this?"

"I might be able to scramble them a little and slow them down," Dent answered, but he didn't look optimistic. "But transmissions started flying all over as soon as we hit the fleet. I've no doubt they've already sent a message home if they intended to."

"So, nothing we can do about it then," Taj griped. "Oh, well. Ready the shuttles. We've got a planet to free before anyone else shows up."

CHAPTER TWO

Just like the armada of ships they'd left in space, the fleet of shuttles that streaked toward Krawlas were automated, controlled by Dent.

The living crew piled into a couple of them and about forty service bots joined them, spread out across the different shuttles to avoid crowding.

Taj gritted her teeth as they broke orbit and entered the atmosphere of Krawlas. She fiddled with the armor on her forearm that hid the foot-long blade. She wondered if she'd have to use it soon.

While she hadn't planned on fighting a ground battle, she hadn't been so ignorant as to think it couldn't happen, so they'd prepared for it. The shuttles were equipped with far more firepower than they normally would be, Dent having readied them to be used for air support while the Furlorian crew made the most of their armored suits.

Taj had had the Furlorians join them, training night and day ever since General Reynolds had agreed to let them go off on their own. The difficulty of the android Wyyvan practice dummies had been ramped up by Dent to simulate a more difficult fight, but even then, the Furlorians were worth five or more of the scaly lizard gacks.

We have to be, Taj thought, considering just how few of them there were on this mission compared to the Wyyvan soldiers they knew would be there. The lizards outnumbered them ten to one by Dent's calculations, although they had no solid intel at this point.

Regardless, Taj and the crew needed every advantage they could get, considering that the numbers were never going to be on their side.

Especially not if the dreadnought had called for help.

The ground approached rapidly as she stared the view screen, seeing her home world up close for the first time in what felt like ages, although it had only been a year.

It had changed dramatically—and not for the better.

While she and the others had only flown the ancient cruiser into space a couple of times while they were training, Taj remembered the view of her home as a stark panorama of reds and browns that had stolen her breath.

It did so again, but for entirely different reasons this time around.

Culvert City, the small town where she and her littermates had been born and raised—an oasis in the desert scrubland that surrounded it— had once sat at the end of Everon's Canyon, but all that had been wiped from the face of Krawlas.

In its place was a cold, walled outpost that sprawled across the stripped land where balborans and Furlorians alike once roamed. The Maladorian Plains that had been home to a host of peaceful creatures now looked like a monstrous beast had dug its claw into the ground and ripped deep, jagged wounds.

It appeared to be ready to expire.

All the balborans were gone, nothing remaining to show that they had ever been there. Taj's stomach churned.

"That's...ugly as all gack," Lina muttered, staring at the Wyyvan mining compound that had replaced their town.

Taj couldn't help but agree.

Long, squat buildings of gray sat where the once rustic brown and reds of the Furlorian barns and homes used to be. There was a regimented rigidity to the buildings that Krawlas had never before hosted. Hard lines replaced the curving dirt roads and winding paths that had run wild through Culvert City.

Black smoke rose from the compound as ground vehicles flitted back and forth, driving through the maze, trailers at their backs, hauling off what Taj could only presume was Toradium-42. Great trenches surrounded the compound in every direction, dusty crevices littered with mining equipment. They were barren of life.

"Where are all the people?" Taj asked.

Her answer came in the form of anti-aircraft fire.

A great wall of energy streaked toward the descending shuttles, and Taj was grateful Dent had made modifications to the shields on the ships, making them more durable and capable.

Anti-aircraft blasts rattled the crew's shuttle as the shields took the brunt of the damage, but there was no mistaking the severity of the attack upon them.

"AA fire is lighting up all across the outpost," Cabe

reported, grimacing, whiskers pinned to his cheeks. "These gacks are ready to fight."

"Can we take them out?" Taj asked.

He shook his head. "They're set up in the population centers, alongside what look like artillery units," he explained. "That's where all the gacking people have gone. Scanners are picking up too many lifeforms stationed nearby to risk it."

"Blast the guns, kill the slaves. Fantastic," Taj growled.

She had known that the Wyyvans were ruthless—Vort and Dard had been perfect examples of that—but she hadn't given the lizards much credit for being intelligent. Taj had underestimated them.

"Lost a shuttle," Cabe called out. "Gack, there goes another one. We're getting shot to pieces hanging out up here above the outpost."

"Target the guns along the perimeter and bring us about toward the Maladorian Plains so we're not dropping down right on top of them. Evasive maneuvers," Taj ordered.

Dent wasted no time responding.

The shuttles veered to the east of the outpost, dodging and weaving and returning fire. Taj's stomach flipped as the ship made sharp, steep maneuvers, the atmosphere of her home planet beating her up with its not-so-welcoming embrace.

Their return shots hit the walls of the outpost, a number of cannons going up in fiery gouts, but it did little to stop the barrage of fire streaking toward them.

"They're firmly entrenched," Dent reported, reading the scanners. "While I'm sure they didn't expect you to come back to reclaim your home, they most certainly planned to hold it should anyone else show up."

"Any way to cloak us?" Taj asked.

The AI shook his head. "The camouflage units on the shuttles are the same as those on your suits, albeit a bit weaker due to the size," he explained. "They work best in crowded terrain where the refractors can latch onto and imitate their surroundings. In open sky like this, moving at the speeds we are, we'd simply look like vessels with gaudy blue and white paint jobs."

"We've lost two more shuttles!" Cabe reported. "Another is taking damage. It's dropping off."

"Spread out and get us on the ground out of range as quickly as you can," Taj commanded. "We can't have these guys picking us off before we get a chance to set foot on-planet."

Once again, the shuttle fleet reacted to Dent's whims. The ships flitted back and forth like a host of gralflies atop a dead balboran, zipping off at odd angles and adjusting their speed to make themselves difficult targets.

It worked.

Taj tasted bile in her throat from the assault of vertigo upon her senses and swallowed it back. She'd be damned if she showed any weakness to the crew right now.

She needed to be strong, to show no fear. They were in it deep, and she'd been the one to talk them into the plan. There was no way she would let them down.

Her teeth clenched as the shuttle leveled off and spun about, giving her a clear view of the outpost in the distance. Anti-aircraft blasts lit the air between them and the gray monstrosity that had been erected in Culvert City's place, but none came near to hitting them.

"We're out of their firing arc now," Dent reported.

"Finally," Torbon moaned.

The barrage began to waver, the onslaught slowing as the enemy realized they were wasting their efforts. It stopped completely a few moments later.

"We lose anyone?" Taj asked.

"Five shuttles and about that many bots," Cabe replied, "but all of our people made it through."

Taj's head lolled back against the headrest and she sighed. "That's good news, at least."

"We do any substantive damage to their weapons?" Taj followed up, straightening in her seat. Now wasn't the time to relax.

"No, not really," Cabe answered, fingers flying over the console. "Took a couple of their anti-aircraft guns out here and there, but there were simply too many of the non-Wyyvan lifeforms around the weapons as cover."

"How'd they know we wouldn't blast them too?" Lina asked.

"They couldn't know," Taj replied.

"Most likely a standard defensive maneuver for the Wyyvans," Dent stated. "The fact that we didn't immediately bombard the planet from space made it a wise choice, though. Had we been looking to raze the outpost, we could have done it as soon as we engaged the Wyyvan fleet. That tells them we want something down here."

"So they already know our tactics?" Taj groaned. "Gacking wonderful."

"We're definitely not dealing with someone like Captain

Vort, then," Torbon muttered. "His lizard-ass would have left his fleet behind to battle it out with us, regardless of the cost."

"Which means this commander is smarter than Vort," Cabe suggested.

"Doesn't take much to earn that honor," Lina joked.

"Maybe not, but what does that make *us* if we walked right into the middle of it?" Taj asked.

Torbon chuckled. "It makes us—"

"Rhetorical question, Torbon," Lina told him, shutting Torbon up before he could put his foot in his mouth. "Doesn't really need an answer."

"Maybe not, but we need to take a look at our circumstances and come up with something quick or the lizards are gonna make us look like gacking idiots compared to Vort. We might not have walked into a Wyyvan trap, but we sure didn't do ourselves any favors by coming down right on top of them like we did."

Taj grunted. "He's right. I made a lot of presumptions before coming here—"

"We all did," Cabe corrected. "We thought we could show up, guns blazing, and take back our world in an afternoon and be lazing in the sun by evening, but that clearly isn't gonna happen. We need a new plan."

"Cabe's right," Lina agreed. "So things didn't work out the way we hoped, so what? We're not gonna let this stop us, are we?"

"Definitely not!" Taj answered, shaking her head.

"Well, whatever we do, we need to get to it quickly," Dent interrupted. "Scanners are showing Wyyvan forces massing near the walls of the outpost on the eastern side.

They're not moving on us yet, but I would imagine it won't be long before they do. They substantially outnumber us."

"Then let's stir up some dust," Taj decided. "Everyone out," she ordered over the comm. "Bots, stay in place."

She triggered the shuttle's exit hatch and left the ship, the crew following her out into the gritty, barren landscape. Her heart ached as the dirt crunched beneath her boots. There was so little remaining of the world they'd left behind. Seeing it as it was sickened her.

"Seal up your suits and get ready to move," she ordered, turning to Dent. "Get these shuttles out of here. Find someplace a short distance away where they'll be safe from artillery and AA fire and can be camouflaged well enough to keep them from being quickly detected."

"You want to strand us?" Torbon asked.

She shook her head. "Just looking to make us harder targets," she told him. "Keep the armada over our heads to warn off the Wyyvan fleet. Engage them if they even start to look our way, or if you see an opportunity. We don't want them picking us off from space," she told the AI. "As for the shuttles, keep them close enough for a quick evac if we need it, and stir up a mess when they leave, making a show of it."

"Won't that give away our location?" Jadie asked.

"They already know it," Dent replied.

"Which is why the launch needs to be messy. The shuttles stir the dirt, and we run the stealth programs on our suits," Taj explained. "As long as the Wyyvan fleet doesn't return to close orbit and start scanning for us, we can essentially disappear down here to the limited-range scanners the soldiers will have available to them."

The shuttles lifted off then, kicking up a massive cloud of dust as Taj had requested. Dirt swirled around the crew, darkening the sky and blacking out the area.

"Let's go," Taj ordered over the comm as soon as she felt there was enough dirt dancing around to obscure their direction of travel.

"You're making me regret deciding to come live with you people," Krawg complained, waving a hand in front of his visor despite the fact that Taj knew he could see perfectly well thanks to the advanced optics. "All this dirt makes me miss the snow."

"At least it's not cold here," Torbon countered.

"I wish it was." Krawg chuckled. "Maybe you've forgotten all the fur I've stuffed inside this suit?"

"Only the smell of it," Torbon fired back, laughing.

Taj ignored the two and raced off, leading the crew across the dusty scrubland and down into a nearby gully. It broke off into a dozen more, sprawling out as if they were branches of a tree.

She picked a direction at random and kept on, pushing to put some distance between the crew and the place they'd set down and moving only in the general direction of the outpost.

She knew a determined effort by the Wyyvans would eventually suss them out, so the soldiers would have to get close before that happened.

At that range, Taj and the crew could inflict massive damage on them before they knew what hit them. She didn't figure they would be that bold, although she had to admit, she'd misjudged a lot of things regarding this mission.

She swore to stop doing that.

Too much rested on her shoulders to screw it up, especially this early in the campaign.

While she'd left the bulk of her people back on Corzant, safe from harm, if Taj and the others failed here, it meant those people would never see their home again. Ever.

Taj wouldn't let that happen.

She'd promised the spirits of Gran Beaux and Mama Merr that she'd fix all this and set things right. But most of all, she'd promised herself.

There was no way she'd let these gacking lizards take their home away twice.

She flitted through the deep gully carefully to avoid kicking up dust and giving away their location. The trenches she moved through were disheartening reminders of how much damage the Wyyvan had done to Krawlas.

Although the land hadn't been much more than desert scrub where they were, it had been mined haphazardly in an effort to collect as much Toradium-42 as they could as quickly as possible.

She presumed the work had been done early on by the lizards, before they'd refined their efforts and figured out how to better mine the mineral under the surface, but seeing it made her sick.

The Wyyvans had torn the ground apart with callous disregard for the flora or fauna that called the desert home, just like they had with the Furlorians.

There'd been no mercy involved.

Taj pressed on, weaving through the gullies, marveling at how deep some of them were. Many ran to four meters, all sizes of dark tunnels shooting off from the walls and disappearing underground. The jagged, scraped ground sparkled with the remnants of the Toradium-42 that had been gouged from the planet.

There was so much of it that it was impossible for the Wyyvans to mine it all.

Taj didn't know whether to be glad or upset about that.

If nothing else, it told her the lizards would do their damndest to maintain their hold on Krawlas no matter what. The mineral was simply too valuable and too abundant to leave behind for someone else to collect.

That meant that even if Taj and the crew succeeded in defeating the Wyyvan contingent on the planet and above, she could be sure more would come back in an effort to retake their claim.

She imagined having to take the fight to the Wyyvan home world one day, and the thought made her head reel. It hadn't been something she'd pictured when planning to take Krawlas back. It certainly wasn't something she'd expected to commit her people to, either.

Taj stumbled to a halt as images of a war-torn future assailed her. She stared up at the sky as Cabe came over and set a hand on her shoulder.

"You okay?" he asked, giving a gentle squeeze.

"Yeah," she replied, shaking off the thought of going to war with the whole of the Wyyvan race. "Was just thinking, working things out," she told him, readying to start off again.

"Picked a bad time to do that," a strange voice announced from above them.

The crew stiffened and spun about to see a female standing over them, a rifle pointed their direction.

Dressed in dusty brown pants with a brownish wrap slung over her torso, her yellow eyes gleamed with ferocity.

"We're not alone," Dent stated.

"No gack," Torbon muttered as dozens of similarly dressed people crept out of the tunnels, weapons up and aimed at the crew.

"Don't move or you die," an older male told them, inching forward.

He looked gaunt, but not frail.

Taj swallowed hard. The weapons were much like the bolt rifles she and the Furlorians had used when they'd roamed Krawlas. They were crude but powerful.

She was sure the armored suits she and the crew wore would protect them to a degree, but there was no certainty no one would get hurt or killed at this close of range. She decided not to take the chance.

Taj eased her hands into the air. "Nobody do anything stupid," she ordered over the comm.

"Like surrender?" Torbon asked, reluctantly raising his hands along with the rest of the crew. "You know we can take these guys, right?"

Glad the suits muted the conversation from those outside, she wondered for a second if Torbon was right, but decided against going on the attack.

No one needed to get hurt.

"Stand down," she ordered.

A quick look at the people surrounding them told her they weren't Wyyvan, and they weren't Furlorian either, so that gave her a pretty good idea as to who they were.

"We're not with the lizards," she announced. "In fact, we're here to kill them."

Taj triggered her helmet, causing it to meld back into her armor, revealing her features. Several of the strangers gasped at seeing her, and she noticed their weapons wavering.

"You're Furlorians?" the older male asked.

Taj nodded. "Most of us, at least," she told him. "We've come to take our planet back."

"Off to a good start, I see," a young female standing behind the older male snapped, sneering at Taj.

Her skin was dark, almost obsidian, and it gleamed beneath the dirt crusted across her face. Brilliant orbs of blue stared at Taj.

"Easy, Rat," another male told her, holding his hand up to quiet her.

"Just stating the obvious, Malcolm," Rat went on, unperturbed by the male's chastising.

"Doesn't mean they aren't who they say they are," Malcolm shot back. "Let's give them a chance to explain things."

"Malcolm's right," the older male said.

"Are you serious, Jak?" Rat asked.

"I am," he answered, not bothering to look at the young female as he did. "Still, I can't say I'm comfortable with you people carrying all that hardware around with you. Hand over those rifles on your backs, and we can find a nice, quiet, out of the way location without lizards around to discuss your future."

"Or we could—"

Taj reached out and thumped Torbon in the chest,

cutting him off before he got his threat out and instigated something.

"Do it," she ordered, easing the rifle off her back.

Seeing as how it was hardly the only weapon she had, the others melded into the armor like her helmet was, she didn't have a problem offering the strangers the most obvious of their armaments.

If that was what it took for them to complete their mission, so be it.

After the weapons were passed over, the strangers ushered them into the nearby tunnels, leading them into the darkness.

CHAPTER THREE

"So, you escaped from the Wyyvans?" Taj asked Jak.

She glanced at her surroundings as he nodded.

The strangers had led them through a maze of narrow tunnels, bringing the crew to a large, rough-hewn cavern several meters beneath the surface of Krawlas. It reminded her of the tunnel system that had been beneath Culvert City. She wondered how much of it was natural, although she was certain these people had put considerable effort into expanding the cave system.

They'd passed one of the Wyyvan tunneling machines on the way in.

"We did," Jak answered, sitting on a rock that had been positioned to be a chair.

Dozens more of the makeshift seats were scattered about, and the crew plopped onto a number of them. Jak's people stood around in a loose circle, guns still pointed at the Furlorians, who'd all removed their helmets to assure the strangers that none of them were Wyyvans in disguise.

"These scaly bastards brought most of us here about ten months or so back from all over the place," Jak went on. "Hard to remember exactly when it was, seeing as how ain't no one scratching reminders in the dirt or anything, but it's been a while now."

"They brought you here to mine for them?" Lina asked.

Jak nodded. "Plan to bring more, too, or so I've heard, but Grand Admiral Galforin, the lizard sack of shit in charge up there on that dreadnought, doesn't appear to be in a hurry to expand his operations for whatever reasons."

"Means more work for us," Rat muttered.

"I remember that name," Cabe growled. "Vort told us about him."

Taj nodded, swallowing the venom she wanted to spew at hearing the lizard's name. He'd been the one to blast Krawlas, answering Captain's Vort's call for backup, killing her people and forcing those who'd survived to flee.

"It's probably because he wants the profit for himself," Dent clarified. "No point in making a big deal of things if it draws attention to what he's doing."

Taj was sure the AI was right.

Just like Vort, the other Wyyvans in command were selfish gackwads who would do anything to get ahead of the rest of their people.

Lina raised her arm to the ceiling, examining the computer attached to her armored forearm as she scanned the room. "I presume the Wyyvans can't pick you up down here because of the Toradium-42."

"Not that they try all that hard," Rat spat out. "We're no threat to them, no matter what Jak wants us to believe."

"Always have to be difficult, huh, Rat?" Malcolm asked, shaking his head.

"Always have to be reasonable," she fired back. "Look at us. We're a bunch of dirt-eaters with blankets for armor. We're not exactly a threat to the lizards, even on a good day."

"We can help with that," Taj offered, seeing an opportunity.

"Yeah, like you and your people didn't get snuck up on and captured by tunnel-crawlers with antique popguns," Rat countered. "What help can you possibly give us?"

Taj grinned.

Then she was on the girl.

Her armored suit pushing her natural speed advantage to its limit, Taj ducked under Rat's weapon and knocked it from her hands with a swipe. As she did that, she ejected her pistol from her suit, pulling it up and around and holding it to the young girl's temple before Rat could so much as gasp.

Taj offered a feral smile. "We're hardly helpless," she explained, letting go of the girl and nudging her forward before Taj returned to her seat, putting her pistol away.

The crowd stirred in response, nervous hands jabbing gun barrels toward the crew, unsure whether to shoot or run away.

"Even without the rifles you took," Taj went on, "we could kill each and every one of you without fear of reprisal."

It took every ounce of Taj's self-control to keep her façade stable, to keep from showing anything to these people that would make them suspect she was bluffing.

The last thing she wanted to do was have to fight or hurt these people, but she was even more concerned by how many of her own people might get hurt were hostilities to break out.

She hoped her posturing would buy them some leverage with the escaped slaves, or at least some information.

Although she and the other Furlorians knew the nature of Krawlas, having been born and raised there, the compound and surrounding area had undergone a drastic transformation. The slaves, however, knew the *current* Krawlas, and that information would be invaluable to Taj if she was to take out the occupying force of Wyyvans.

Rat ran over and grabbed her rifle from the ground and came back, jabbing it in Taj's face.

Taj sat stoically, staring down the wavering barrel of the weapon.

"Put it away, Rat," Jak told the girl. "They proved their point, that's all."

The young female stood there with a trembling sneer on her lips. Taj was worried that Rat might just pull the trigger and be done with it, but the girl eased back at last, stepping away, although she didn't lower the rifle.

"You ever touch me again—" Rat let the threat hang.

Taj nodded to the girl, hoping to earn her respect. "Fair enough. Was only a demonstration."

Rat was tough, clearly, and headstrong and brave, and Taj didn't want to do anything to discourage that. They would need allies like her in the fight ahead.

"Go get a drink, Rat," Jak ordered. "Take a minute to catch your breath."

Rat held her ground long enough to make it clear it was her choice to leave, not Jak's, then she sashayed off, glaring at Taj the entire time.

"Looks like you've made a friend already," Torbon said over the comm, covering his mouth so no one but the crew heard him. "Should probably watch your back from now on. That kid looks fierce."

"You'll have to forgive Rat—" Jak started, but Taj cut him off with a wave.

"Nothing to forgive. She doesn't know us, so she's only being smart," Taj explained. "She has nothing to prove to us."

"I'm glad you understand," Jak went on. "If we're honest, though, I agree with Rat. While you might have fancy armor and weapons, you're not exactly an invasion force, which raises a lot of questions as to why you're really here." He motioned to the small number of crew present. "The only reason we didn't kill you after we captured you was because you're Furlorian."

"Why did that buy us your mercy?" Cabe asked, barely restraining his anger at the attitudes of these people.

"Because we've proven ourselves to them," a hauntingly familiar voice said from the shadows.

Taj and the crew leapt to their feet and stared at the source, eyes wide and mouths gaping.

"Harley?" Taj asked.

The young girl stepped forward, offering them a soft smile. An older tom stood beside her, looking sullen.

She recognized them both from when Mama Merr had passed on. The pair of them had been in the tunnels with her when it happened.

Both looked gaunt; far thinner than she remembered them.

"I thought—"

"We were dead?" Harley asked, no hint of rancor in her voice. "We pretty much were," she went on. "Me and Garr here were caught in the catacombs when the Wyyvans started bombing Culvert City."

"Wasn't anywhere to go," Garr finished. "The lizards dug us out a few days later and put us to work."

Taj's blood froze in her veins. She stumbled forward, a hand over her mouth. "I'm so…sorry."

Harley wrapped her in a hug, pulling Taj close. "Don't be," she replied, shaking her head. "You had everyone else to worry about. You did the right thing."

Garr nodded his agreement as the two separated. "Beaux would be proud to see you now."

While Taj had managed to hold back her emotions, the mention of Beaux nudged her over the top. A tear ran down her cheek, and Taj wiped it away with the back of her hand.

Now wasn't the time to be crying.

"How many of you…" she started.

"About fifteen of us," Harley answered, "although many of those were the older Grans." She sighed. "They didn't make it long under the Wyyvans' whips."

Harley's words were like a blow to Taj's face.

"There are ten of us now," Harley continued, "but only me and Garr here managed to escape the outpost."

"The rest are still trapped inside?" Lina asked, not holding back her emotions as well as Taj was. Tears glistened in her eyes.

Garr nodded. "We've been trying to get them out, along with everyone else, but it's not like we're prepared to take the fight to the lizards. Gack, we barely get by day to day, scavenging off the land now that all the balborans have been slaughtered."

Taj growled. It was bad enough that she had left people behind, but to realize they had been made into slaves and were likely starving made her stomach churn with disgust.

It was just one more atrocity she intended to hold the Wyyvans accountable for.

"We can fix this," she stated unequivocally. "We *will* fix this."

She spun around to face Dent.

"Have a bot load up rations from the shuttles and sneak them this way as soon as it's safe. And some blankets and clothing—whatever we have that these people can use," she added.

Dent nodded, and Taj knew he'd send the order without giving any indication of doing so.

"That's nice and all…" Jak interrupted, "and we appreciate it, be sure of that, but we can use more help than hand-me-downs and treats."

"We plan to do much more," Torbon bragged.

"You going to kill all the Wyyvans?" Malcolm asked.

"With my own bare hands if necessary," Torbon assured him, clenching his armored hands into fists. "The gacking lizards need to die."

"It's one thing to say it," Jak told him, "but it's something else entirely to pull it off." He motioned to the crew again. "Like I was saying before, you're not exactly an

37

army. You a scout force? The rest of your people in orbit, waiting for a signal?"

"We're all there is," Taj answered, deciding not to lie, "but that doesn't mean we can't do this."

"No, maybe not," Jak replied, obviously disappointed, "but I have to say, with less than forty of you, I find it hard to be confident you can turn things around."

"I don't like this," Malcolm admitted.

"Neither do I," Jak said. "You've stirred up the lizards, got them looking to the desert after we finally got them to look away. They're going to make a concentrated push to find you soon." Jak glanced at the tavern's ceiling. "Tell me you at least took out the Wyyvan fleet before you landed."

"Sent them running," Torbon bragged, grinning.

"They're still there, though," Taj finished.

Jak and Malcolm sighed in unison.

"You ain't filling me with joy, Cat," Malcolm muttered.

"We didn't come here to save you," Cabe fired back. "Didn't even know you people were here. We'd planned to blast the gacks from space and retake our home, but we realized there were hostages here and decided to come down to try and rescue you. The least you can do is help us help you."

Jak grunted. "All that passion don't mean shit if you don't have the firepower to back it up, boy," he said. "We appreciate the sentiment, but sentiment isn't going to keep us from getting killed.

"You're likely dead anyway if we don't succeed," Krawg said from his seat, always the voice of obnoxious reason.

All eyes turned to him, Jak and Malcolm's expressions shifting to glares.

He shrugged. "Those ugly looks you're giving me doesn't change the truth," he told them. "How long do you people think you'll last here?"

"We've done all right so far," Malcolm shot back.

"So far," the huge Ursite repeated, "you've done well, looks like. But ten months is nothing. Look at how little the Wyyvans have accomplished in that time."

He pointed at the ceiling, implying the land above.

"They've hardly scratched the surface with their mining efforts," he went on. "And you said it yourself: that Wyyvan admiral hasn't been in a hurry to expand. But he will, you can be sure of that."

"That's *your* fault," Malcolm shouted.

"Probably," Krawg replied with a shrug, getting to his feet and towering over the old male, "but nothing can be done about that now."

Taj saw the flutter of Krawg's upper lip and decided to step in. The Ursite wasn't one to take disrespect lightly even though he was willing to offer it, and Taj could see Malcolm's frustration getting him—and them—into an unnecessary conflict.

"He's right," Taj said, stepping in front of Krawg to draw everyone's attention. "The Wyyvans are gonna escalate things now that we've shown up and brought the fight to them. It's not gonna matter who's responsible soon enough."

"You're forcing our hands," Jak stated.

"Not intentionally," Taj replied.

"But that doesn't matter," Dent cut in. "What's done is done, and there's no winding it back, sorry to say. As such, it's in your best interests, and ours, to help us free the rest of the slaves so we can blast the Wyyvans to dust from orbit before reinforcements show up."

"You mean like the fleet that's still up there?" Jak growled. "It's only a matter of time until those ships come back looking for blood. The fact that you didn't destroy them already means you probably can't, or am I wrong about that?"

"I'm not gonna lie," Taj began. "We didn't expect the Wyyvan to be so entrenched, and we didn't come prepared to take on such a huge force of ships. But we're not without our own resources, and I'm not leaving this planet under Wyyvan occupation."

"That's all well and good, like your boy there, but I'm not hearing anything that makes me think we'd be signing up with the winning side if we back you," Jak returned. "You get credit for determination and grit, but that ain't no substitute for numbers and overwhelming firepower."

Taj hated to admit that the male was right.

For all her promises to herself or anyone else, there was still a cold, hard reality she had to address. But she hadn't come all this way to fail.

"Look, maybe you're right. We aren't the army you'd been hoping for, and maybe we *did* poke the ferion spider sack by showing up the way we did…"

Torbon shuddered. "I hate those things."

"…but we are your best chance of escaping this planet alive," Taj told the male. "Still, I understand your reluctance. But work with us; meet us halfway, at least. We can do this."

"What does halfway look like to you?" Jak asked.

"Let's work together to free the rest of the slaves from

the Wyyvan yoke and get them out of the compound before the lizards hit back, and even if we have to retreat…"

The rest of the crew turned to stare at her.

"…for now, we'll take you off-planet and drop you somewhere while we regroup and figure out the bigger battle on our own."

"That still puts us at risk," Malcolm complained.

"You already are," Krawg stated, staring back at him.

"You don't have to help us," Cabe added, spitting out a stream of brown nip juice, "but we're moving forward regardless." He jabbed a finger at the ground. "This is *our* planet, and we plan to take it back, no matter what. If you're not gonna help, then stay outta the way."

Taj was amazed by Cabe's ferocity.

He'd been worked up and excited as they'd planned and plotted to reclaim Krawlas, but she hadn't seen him so forceful and passionate about the idea.

Being home had clearly inspired him to take Krawlas back.

"Not that you've left us much choice," Malcolm grunted.

"I'm in," Rat said, coming back over to the group with her chin defiantly in the air. "If there's a chance we can get through this, I'm betting on them." She gestured to Taj and the crew.

Taj bit back a sigh. She'd clearly rattled the young female enough to spur her into action.

Now, if only she could do the same for the others.

"We're running out of time," Taj explained, pushing the

point. "With or without you, we have a mission to accomplish."

Jak sighed. He waved to his people, gesturing for them to put their weapons away. Most of them had already, Taj noticed, which was a good sign.

"We'll meet you halfway, then," Jak said. "We'll help you get into the outpost and get as many people clear as we can, but I'm not committing anyone to anything beyond that. Then you get us off-planet."

Taj nodded her agreement to the terms.

She had no intention of abandoning Krawlas to the Wyyvans again, but she needed to take things one step at a time. Freeing the slaves was the first priority, then she could worry about what they did after that.

But when all was said and done, she would have her home back.

CHAPTER FOUR

"Scanner reports from the *Decimator* tell me the Wyyvan fleet is moving into a defensive formation around the temporary Gate they set up," Dent relayed. "They appear to be making room around the Gate."

"Likely preparing for reinforcements," Lina said, snarling at the thought.

"Some rescue attempt this is," Rat muttered, only half-joking.

Taj grunted. It wasn't a friendly alliance, but it was still an alliance. She kept her mouth shut to keep from setting off the young female they'd only barely managed to get on their side.

"We still have time," Dent assured everyone. "There's no buildup of energy at the Gate, which tells me the maneuver is little more than posturing at this point."

"You better hope so," Malcolm growled.

"That the fleet isn't advancing is a good sign," Dent said.

"It means they're still unsure what level of threat we actually pose."

"That's all well and good until these lizards here…" Jak rose from behind the small sand dune they lurked behind to point at the nearby outpost, "poke their heads out and take a looksee and realize we number less than a hundred bodies, all told. Then they'll radio their admiral and bring his fleet down on our head."

"That won't be happening anytime soon." Dent shook his head. He pulled a small device out of his suit. "Now that I'm close enough, I've set up a transmission block, keeping the Wyyvans down here from reaching out to their fleet until they go back overhead."

Dent stuffed the device into the sand, burying it.

"This will keep them blind and out of touch for a little while," Dent announced.

"You've got all *sorts* of fancy toys, don't you?" Malcolm asked.

Taj wasn't sure if it was sarcasm or awe the male was expressing, but she figured it might be a little of both given the conflicted look on Malcolm's face.

"For all our errors, we came prepared to win the planet back," Dent said casually. "We intend to do exactly that."

"Well, let's hope it's enough," Jak answered. He gestured toward the great, gray wall of the outpost. "They've got anti-aircraft units all along the ridge of the wall, but like you noticed when you came in, the majority of the artillery pieces are spread out through the main outpost itself, set right among the people they'd gathered to use as shields."

"That's what kept us from taking them out," Cabe growled.

"Nice to know you have a conscience," Malcolm told him, "but these lizards sure don't. They'll kill their workers without hesitation if they think it'll buy them an extra minute or two."

"We've seen their cruelty up close and personal," Taj stated, snarling. "We've no plan to let them exhibit it again."

"What you want to happen and what *will* happen are two different things, Cat," Jak replied. "We pop out too close to that wall and they'll rain down hell on us, artillery and small arms fire to boot. Maybe those AA guns, too."

Taj nodded. She could see the solid line of defenses on the wall, and while she believed she and her crew could pierce them if they decided to assault the outpost, it wouldn't be without great loss.

She wasn't willing to go that route.

Her gaze drifted along the wall as Jak pointed out different aspects of the Wyyvan outpost, but from where they were hunkered, there was little she could actually determine.

"I need to get closer," she announced. "I can't see anything clearly from way back here."

"How you planning on doing that?" Rat asked.

Taj triggered her suit's stealth mode and smiled as the young girl stumbled back, covering her mouth.

"The toys Malcolm mentioned have their uses," she answered, grinning. "Dent, Cabe, Torbon, Lina, Krawg, come with me. The rest of you, stay put and out of sight. We'll be back shortly."

"Nice to know I drew the short straw without even picking one," Torbon complained, but he activated his suit's camouflage anyway.

TIM MARQUITZ

"That's strange," Rat mumbled, her eyes narrowed as she tried to take in the whole of the camouflaged crew. Taj could tell she was having a hard time despite being so close. The only thing she could see clearly were their heads, since none of them had their helmets sealed.

Taj waved and sealed her suit, the others following her actions. Then she darted off without another word.

Time was running out and she could feel the pressure mounting, but she wasn't going to let it get the better of her and make her do something stupid.

Too many people were counting on her.

No, too many people were counting on *them*— the crew. This was a team effort, and although she was in charge and the burden of failure was on her shoulders, she wasn't alone. *They* would see this through.

Taj had to remember to think of it that way. This wasn't about her.

She crept across the barren scrubland, sticking to the lower areas where only the barest remnants of shrubs had begun to return to the savaged land. Fortunately, in the rush to dig up the Toradium-42, the lizards had torn great crevices in the ground almost all the way up to the wall of the outpost itself.

While they'd been smart enough to leave a narrow killing field that made it almost impossible to sneak up on the outpost without being seen—at least without the aid of Dent's technology—the Wyyvan had gacked up by leaving so much cover available.

Taj crept to within twenty meters of the wall before she decided it was too much of a risk to barrel into the field without surveying it first.

She hunkered down and used her suit's optics to scan the surrounding area and the Wyyvans on the wall.

"I'm picking up a mass of soldiers near the doorway there. Same ones I noted earlier," Dent reported, motioning toward a massive sliding door that seated into the wall, leaving just a crack to show it was even there. "No furtive motions. Looks as if they are posted there as a precaution," he reported.

"So, they haven't seen us sneaking around out here," Cabe said, sighing. "That's good news."

"As long as we're not trying to go through the door, that is," Torbon added.

"Why don't you do that and distract them?" Krawg asked, grinning broadly, his sharpened teeth gleaming. "I'll back you up."

"You first, Furry," Torbon fired back.

"Quit it before I shoot both of you and save the Wyyvan the effort," Taj warned.

Torbon shrugged. "Wouldn't be the first time."

"Why do I even bother?" Taj groaned.

"Been meaning to ask you that," Cabe joked.

She shook her head and took a few moments to track the movement of the lizards on the wall. Once she had their timing down, she hunkered back down and faced the crew.

"Are there scanners on the wall, Dent?" she asked.

He took a moment to double-check and shook his head. "The place is quite low-tech," he answered. "Seems the Wyyvans haven't gone out of their way to upgrade the basic infrastructure beyond the bare necessities."

"No point, when they plan on razing the place and

leaving it in ruin once they're finished with it," Cabe remarked.

"That and the fact that I suspect they don't want to attract attention by giving off too many energy signals," Dent added. "They don't want anyone else stumbling onto their find and helping themselves."

"They won't be around long enough for that to matter," Cabe assured the AI, growling.

Hyper-aware of how precious their time was, Taj decided it was time to get moving. "Okay, I want to see what we're looking at inside the place before we do anything," she told them.

"Jak's given you the basic layout, right?" Lina asked.

"Yeah, but I'm not sold on his help just yet. He didn't exactly offer it willingly," she admitted. "I can't see him giving us up to the Wyyvans since the lizards aren't gonna trade with him. They'd kill him and his people out of spite, no matter what they brought them. Still, I can see him feeding us to them indirectly if it buys him and his people time. With us gone, the Wyyvans go back to business as usual and forget about them."

"You think Jak would do that?" Lina wondered. Her whiskers fluttered pensively.

"I don't know anything at this point, but I'm not taking any chances," Taj answered. "I'd be more inclined to trust him if he and his people were to go in with us and share the danger, but until then, I'm not gonna risk our being held up as a sacrifice to get them off the hook."

"That's awfully cynical of you," Krawg told her. Then he grinned. "I'm proud of you. You're learning."

Taj wasn't sure she was proud of herself. She hated

being so distrusting of people, but she'd seen too much of late not to let it color her view of the world.

"Not who I want to be," she admitted, "but my job is to ensure that all of us are safe. I'll save as many of these people as I can, but I'm not gonna get us killed to do it."

The words left a sour taste in her mouth.

Is this what I'm becoming?

No. Not yet, at least.

She hadn't lost all of her compassion, and Rowl willing, she never would. She simply understood that there was a large amount of gray in the world, squeezed in between the black and white. And the more she experienced out in the universe, the more she realized she would have to skirt the line more often than she liked.

But she swore she'd never cross it.

"Regardless, stay put while I look around," she ordered, not wanting to dwell on the realities of her new life.

She waited a moment longer, watching the guards go about their rounds, and when it was clear, she shot off across the barren field. When she reached the wall, she pressed herself against it, glad she'd thought to check if there were scanning devices there.

The cold of the stone couldn't penetrate her armor, but she imagined it was there and a chill skittered down her spine as she waited.

She counted down, having memorized the timing of the Wyyvan soldiers above, and when she felt safe, she spun around and scrambled up the wall, using the armor's built-in climbing gear.

At the top, she waited again, then shot across the narrow parapet and into the compound. She dropped to the ground inside the wall and darted into the shadows cast by two small buildings that were squeezed close together.

She hadn't wanted to do all this in the daylight, but circumstances had left her little choice. The suit's camo program was impressive, but there was still a chance she could be detected without the cover of night to amplify its effectiveness. But what could she do?

With that in mind, she crept through the streets, ducking or dodging every time someone walked past or she heard a vehicle close by. She realized quickly that the slaves didn't walk the streets alone, and she wondered if that was something recent that had been put in place after the escape of the others or if it had always been that way.

She presumed the former, since it would make it damn impossible for the workers to slip away under the constant eye of the guards.

When Taj examined the place, she realized the vehicles were automated and they seemed to be running a circuit, picking up loads of Toradium-42 and dropping it off somewhere she couldn't see from where she sat.

It gave her an idea how she could speed her reconnaissance up, however.

She lurked in an alley until she spied a loaded vehicle. The streets were clear of Wyyvans, so she bolted out and dove under the vehicle, latching onto the undercarriage and pulling herself tight against it.

The vehicle bounced along, unaware of her presence, and she grinned.

She couldn't have pictured doing something so reckless before, but with the powered suit keep her protected, hidden, and her limbs from tiring, the maneuver was a simple one.

She likened it to the trrilac herding she and the crew participated in every year. *Won't be long before they're back,* she thought, remembering how the Wyyvan ship had crashed just after they'd turned the herd aside, keeping it from tearing apart Culvert City.

Chastising herself for letting her mind drift, Taj shook the reverie clear and went back to noting the layout of the outpost and the arrangement of the artillery units that kept anyone from approaching the compound too closely.

She let the suit record her passage so she could review it later—well, Dent could review it—and pick out anything that would speed up the recovery of the workers and get them the gack out of there.

The vehicle paused only long enough to have an automated device shovel tons of Toradium-42 into the back of the vehicle, Taj's perch rumbling as it did, and then stopped once it reached its destination.

Which was a walled-in chute that protected a conveyor belt with scoops.

The vehicle dumped its load and the conveyor carried it out of sight. Then, not more than a moment later, the vehicle was back on the road, trundling toward the pickup location.

Taj rode it around twice to be sure there wasn't more to the route than she'd seen the first time around and dropped off near the same alley she'd hopped on at.

Back in the shadows, she hunkered down and assessed what she'd seen.

It wasn't good.

The main doorway was the only real entrance or exit to the outpost. All of the Toradium-42 was apparently shunted over the wall into a huge open area in the far corner of the outpost. From there, the machines loaded it and sent it on its way.

She hadn't seen the outside machinery working because the Furlorians' arrival had forced everyone inside, she suspected, but it was kind of obvious how it all worked.

The process was simple, at least as far as she could see, but she could imagine dozens of ways it could be streamlined.

That made her think that Dent was correct in his assessment of Grand Admiral Galforin's intentions.

Like Vort before him, the admiral wanted as much of the mineral as he could hoard before he attracted attention to himself.

She imagined Captain Vort would have done the exact same thing if he hadn't crashed on the planet and had no way off. As it was, he had tried to steal the mineral out from under his superiors anyway.

That was likely why Galforin hadn't cared when he first came to Krawlas, blasting Furlorians and Wyyvans alike. He didn't want any competition for the prize, and that was what Vort had been.

Taj grinned at the thought.

If that were the case, she and her crew might have more time than they imagined.

She couldn't picture Galforin being quick to report recent events to his bosses, given what she'd learned from Vort and Dard about the Wyyvan mentality, so he'd likely have to be more circumspect about finding reinforcements.

And if that were true, Taj could picture being able to take a little more time and do things right rather than rushing them and putting everyone at risk.

Bolstered by that, she slunk back up the wall and made ready to slither down the other side when her armor's sensors picked up a sound she didn't recognize.

She froze and looked around, realizing the soldiers on the wall had hunkered down into their shelters, leaving her alone atop the parapet.

Rather than sit there, she eased over the wall and started down as the sound continued, growing louder with every passing moment.

"You hear that, Dent?" she asked over the comm.

"I do, but I'm not sure what—" The AI's voice cut off and Taj checked her comm, wondering if it had gone out, but the suit's diagnostics showed it was fine.

Dent came back a second later. "Get out of there! Now!"

Explosions tore up the ground near where the rest of the crew had been hiding, and Taj sucked in a sharp breath.

Something shrieked overhead, a flash of silver that cast a cold shadow over her

CHAPTER FIVE

Grand Admiral Galforin fumed, stomping back and forth on the bridge of his dreadnought, the *Stormfront.*

"Have you reestablished communications with the planet yet?" he stopped long enough to ask his communications officer, glaring at the male before resuming his pacing.

"No, sir!" Ensign Huh replied. "Transmissions continue to be blocked. We're working on breaking the coding."

"I suggest you hurry," Galforin warned. He wasn't in the mood to be patient.

Whoever these attackers were, they had come out of nowhere and engaged the grand admiral's fleet without warning or obvious explanation.

Unsure what their goals or capabilities were, he'd ordered the fleet to retreat so he could assess the enemy, but doing so had only made matters worse.

While they pulled back, the enemy fleet had launched

an armada of shuttles, sending them down to the planet's surface. Blocked from scanning them as they descended, Galforin could only imagine they were filled with soldiers staging an invasion.

His inability to confirm that with his troops on the ground infuriated him.

He hated being cut off. Galforin barely maintained his composure and kept from ordering his fleet back into firing range. Although his XO, Volg, suggested they hadn't felt the full measure of the enemy fleet's power, Galforin was uncertain that was true. Why would they attack and not wipe the entire fleet out if they were capable?

It made no sense to leave an enemy behind to come at you again, especially one as powerful as Galforin's fleet.

Yet, he found himself listening to Volg's advice because the XO had been with him since the admiral's start. Volg had been instrumental in Galforin's advance, although he was unsure if the man's patient approach was the correct one given the circumstances they currently found themselves in.

"I don't like this, Volg," Galforin told his XO.

"Nor do I, Admiral," the XO replied, "but there is no reason for the enemy to initiate a ground assault unless they have an understanding of what lies on the planet's surface, sir."

Galforin hissed, licking his lips, his tongue flicking.

It infuriated him that Volg was right, and it flew in the face of Galforin's desire to exact revenge upon the upstarts who dared attack him so boldly.

What made it worse was that he had no idea as to who the enemy fleet belonged to.

None of the ships bore any obvious insignia or were of a design that allowed him to determine who the attackers were.

They could be pirates for all he knew, or agents of Captain Vort, for that matter.

Galforin chuckled.

No, they wouldn't be that.

The admiral recalled hearing the report of one of his scout ships stumbling across the remains of Captain Vort—a frozen, shriveled husk floating in space. The Furlorians who'd escaped the planet and stolen a leech ship had apparently grown tired of the captain and had killed him, ejecting him into space with the tracking device that allowed Galforin to follow the ship.

It had been a bittersweet moment to be sure, Galforin recalled. Though he hated to lose the leech craft since it represented his failure to wipe out the local pest who'd dare defy him, finding Vort that way had been quite amusing, he had to admit.

Galforin had hoped the bastard had been killed by Galforin's assault on KI1047-32—or "Krawlas," as the star registry noted it had been named in recent years—but that hadn't happened, obviously.

Still, it was pleasant to learn that Vort had met a cruel and spiteful end, even if it had been at the hands of someone else.

Galforin had been tempted to order his people to collect the body and return it to him, but he'd decided the captain's fate was the perfect end to the man's treachery and designs at sidestepping Galforin.

So thinking, he let the bastard drift, bound to spend

eternity flying through space, a wretched, soulless, frozen corpse.

"How long before the troops arrive, Volg?" Galforin asked, shaking off the pleasant memories of Vort's death.

"Our people are being circumspect, sir," XO Volg answered. "I've made it clear they must hurry, but there is no clear timeline for their arrival without inadvertently drawing the attention of Command."

Grand Admiral Galforin growled.

Too much rode upon stealth; it frustrated him to have to be so careful.

He'd been glad that Captain Vort had reached out to Galforin directly after his accidental discovery of the mineral on KI1047-32. Had he reported the finding to Command, then the Toradium-42 would have been stolen out from under him—like he'd done with Vort.

He clenched his fists at the thought.

It was far too valuable to allow Command to come in and take it away. He needed only a little longer to collect enough of the valuable mineral to assert his right to a position on the Command Council.

With a planet of the resource, he could buy his way to the top of Command and never have to bow to their wishes again. He would rule Belor Prime, and he could spend his days basking in luxury and the adoration of his inferiors—as long as he could control the planet.

But first, he needed to stop these upstart invaders and bleed them into the sands of the desolate orb that was worth so much.

"Sitrep!" Galforin called, although he'd been informed only moments ago.

"The enemy fleet remains in orbit around KI1047-32, Admiral," XO Volg replied. "No changes of note."

Galforin stopped his pacing, turning to look at his XO. An idea struck him.

"Perhaps it's time to force a change," he suggested. "How effective are the scanners on the Vipers?"

"The fighters are limited in range, Admiral," Volg answered. "I assume you want them for a more accurate assessment of the enemy on the surface of KI1047-32. If so, given the signal blocking, they would need to be right on the enemy for an accurate read."

"That is exactly what I want from them," Galforin replied. "How long would it take them to reach the planet?"

"Minutes, at most," Volg replied, "although it would be best to route them around the planet so as to disrupt any tracking of them by the enemy fleet. That would take a short while longer."

Galforin grinned. "Then do that. Send a cadre of Vipers out immediately, Volg. I want eyes on these would-be usurpers."

XO Volg nodded. "Orders relayed, sir."

The grand admiral drew in a deep breath, reveling in the moist air the *Stormfront's* life support provided. He hated the dry, hot air of KI1047-32, which was why he'd remained aboard his dreadnought rather than oversee the mining operation directly. He didn't know how anyone could stand to exist there.

He grinned as he watched the blips of the Vipers launching on the scanners.

In just a few minutes, if the invaders weren't already burdened by the heat of KI1047-32, they would be.

CHAPTER SIX

Taj watched as a second Wyyvan fighter shrieked overhead. She thought to stay put, hunker down and let the camouflage system do its job, but it didn't take more than a second to realize the fighter had already pinpointed her.

"Camo doesn't work," she screamed as she dove away. The ground was ripped apart and shredded behind her as the fighter zipped past.

"Kinda figured that out," Torbon shouted back over the comm, his breathing fast.

More explosions tore at the dune where the rest of the crew had been hiding. Her advanced optics showed her they had bailed in time, escaping death at the hands of the first Wyyvan pilot.

But it had been close.

The crew scrambled to their feet and scattered to make themselves harder to hit, but out in the open as they were, there wasn't much comfort in it. They were sitting targets in the barren fields, nowhere to hide or take cover.

"Two more incoming," Dent reported.

"Gacking great!" Taj griped as the two Wyyvan fighter craft appeared, strafed the ground, and roared by, veering away sharply to prepare for another pass.

"Air support would be nice," Taj called over the comm.

"Shuttles inbound," Dent came back immediately, "but they're not exactly designed to go one on one with fighters like these."

"And we are?" Torbon asked.

"Good point," the AI admitted.

By then, the first of the fighters had swung around for another shot at the crew.

Taj wasn't going to take the attempt sitting down.

Leading the craft with her pistol sights, she loosed a barrage of fire as soon as the ship cleared the outpost's wall. Blaster shots burst against the hull, kicking up sparks.

Too bad it was like throwing rocks at the planet.

The fighter's armor shrugged off the attack, but the unexpectedness of it surprised the pilot enough to distract him.

His return fire was way off the mark, tearing up the dirt a good five yards from where Taj stood.

She breathed a sigh of relief at that, although it was a pyrrhic victory at best.

"That was ineffective," Krawg muttered.

"Thanks for stating the obvious," Taj growled as the second fighter cleared the outpost and veered off after Dent. "You and Cabe are getting good at that."

Taj's heart thundered against her ribs as she watched

the AI feint a leap in one direction only to dart back her way.

She had to give the Dandrinite's form credit: it was graceful.

Dent rolled and came back to his feet with acrobatic ease as the fighter flew overhead, his weapons fire kicking up clouds of dust and debris well away from where Dent stood.

"We can't keep doing this," the AI warned, and Taj knew he was right.

Fast as they were in their suits, they would eventually slow down or make a mistake, and that would be the end of them.

"How far out are the shuttles?" she asked.

"They'll be here shortly, but as I said earlier, they're not going to be much assistance," he replied. "They'll have to contend with the remaining AA guns shortly."

"They'll risk shooting their own ships to get at ours?" Lina asked.

"I wouldn't put anything past them," Taj answered, remembering just how vicious Vort had been.

The captain would have sacrificed all of his people to take down his enemies. As long as he still stood when the dust cleared, he didn't care what the win cost him.

She didn't imagine Grand Admiral Galforin would be much different.

The fighters were resources to be used up, and they were well worth the cost if they took out the Furlorians.

"Gacking Rowl!" Taj cursed as the third fighter came at her.

She leapt back toward the wall as it ripped up the

ground just ahead of her. The plink of debris against her armor set off warning alarms across the visor display, and she sighed.

Too close, she thought.

"We need to do something soon," Cabe said, stating the obvious.

"What the gack do you want us to do?" Torbon whined. "Wrestle the things?"

Realizations struck Taj, and she grinned.

She imagined she looked a bit feral just then, but given the thoughts flashing through her mind, she felt that it was fitting.

"That's a great idea," she called back, and even she could hear the maniacal tone in her voice.

"Wait, what?" Cabe replied. She knew he was shaking his head, trying to figure out what she meant.

"Don't do anything stupid, Taj," Lina begged, knowing damn well that was exactly what Taj planned.

"I wouldn't call it reckless so much as crazy," Taj fired back, grinning.

She didn't give herself time to second-guess her choice as another of the fighters screamed past the outpost's wall.

Coming in low to do as much damage as possible, the Wyyvan craft was just above the crew's location. With her advanced optics, she could see the lizard pilot smiling in the cockpit, gleefully desperate to be the one to take out the Furlorians and earn his admiral's praise.

"Gack that!" Taj called. "Ain't gonna happen."

She leapt into the air ahead of the fighter as it fired at the ground where she'd just been.

The smile disappeared from the pilot's face as he realized what she'd done.

But it was too late.

With the power of her suit flinging her into the air, Taj rose before the craft and just managed to clear its nose as it streaked beneath her. She howled in disbelief that she'd pulled the maneuver off.

Then she screamed in agony as the cockpit clipped her foot and sent her tumbling.

"Taj!" Cabe screamed in her ears. The sound was a blur of indistinct static; her head spun along with her body.

Her stomach did somersaults and the world whipped past her visor, a blur of gray, brown, and red like a swirl of paint slathering across her vision.

She tumbled head over heels as the Wyyvan fighter flew away and Taj found herself in open air, caught up in the wake of the craft, spinning out of control.

"Well, that clearly didn't work," Krawg muttered over the comm.

That was an understatement, Taj thought as she struggled to right herself and figure out which way was up.

A second later, she found a marker to gauge her positioning.

Unfortunately, it was another of the Wyyvan fighters, which shrieked toward her, engines roaring.

She caught a glimpse of the pilot as he gaped, clearly wondering how the gack she'd ended up in the air with him.

He didn't have time to process the scene, let alone react, before he was right on top of her.

He was so shocked that he didn't even try to shoot her, even though she was a helpless target dead in his sights.

That was a mistake.

Taj twisted as he closed, throwing her entire body into the move.

Her armor responded perfectly, and she slammed into the hull of the fighter just behind where the pilot sat, craning his neck to stare wide-eyed at her through the cockpit's shielding.

Taj clawed at the metallic hull, but the armor was too thick for her fingers to penetrate.

She growled and thumped against the hull, bouncing as the ship's momentum threatened to dislodge her. The craft's tail was coming up behind her; she only had seconds before she collided with it.

Taj knew what would happen then.

If the impact didn't kill her, it would send her careening out of control. As high up as she was, she didn't figure the fall would kill her so much as break her apart.

Splat!

She ignored her mind's sarcastic attempt at humor and pawed at the hull again, desperate to find purchase.

Her fingers found a vent, and she clasped it with all her might.

She thought her shoulder might rip free of its socket as the powered armor caught.

Taj screamed as fire tore the length of her arm, down her shoulder, and across her back, but she held fast.

The fighter pulled up and shot away, the ground hurtling by underneath.

Taj went along for the ride.

"Are you seriously straddling a fighter craft?" Torbon called over the comm.

"Like riding a trrilac," she answered, although it was anything but.

The giant winged beasts were fast, but they were nothing compared to the speed of a fighter as it circled for another around for another pass.

It hadn't quite sunk in yet that the pilot had a hitchhiker.

He glanced behind him as the craft banked, most likely thinking he'd whipped past Taj as though she were an insect, but there she clung, not more than a meter behind him.

The pilot gaped, and Taj knew she only had a split-second before instinct took over and the guy made evasive maneuvers to shake her off his ship.

But who the gack trained for melee while piloting a fighter?

This particular Wyyvan sure hadn't.

He simply stared, unable to comprehend the fact that Taj hung from his hull just behind his cockpit.

She watched the war between reason and insanity going on behind his eyes.

Taj didn't wait to see which won.

Ignoring the burning pain that had engulfed the entire left side of her body, she triggered the blade on her right forearm. It ejected cleanly, gleaming silver in the sunlight.

The sight of it seemed to spur something in the lizard's brain and he whipped around in his seat, pawing at the throttle.

He'd finally processed that she was really there, and he needed to shake her off.

She didn't give him the chance.

Taj swiped her blade in a wide arc, cutting through the shielding at the back of the cockpit.

It gave way easily, metal struts and plastiglas parting in the blade's wake.

The back half of the canopy creaked and broke loose from the front. It clanged off Taj's armored back, nearly dislodging her, but she held on.

Nothing was going to stop her now. She'd risked too gacking much to fail.

She heard the pilot screaming over the shriek of the wind and she figured he was begging his compatriots for help, but there was nothing they could do.

Despite the pain that radiated along her side, she yanked hard and pulled herself forward, nearly leaping into the now-open cockpit.

The pilot went to spin the fighter, but he was too late.

Taj sank her blade through his back.

Blood sprayed her visor, and she twisted her wrist as the blade tore through the lizard and slammed into the controls in front of him. Sparks exploded and flashed past her face as she ripped her weapon free of the dead Wyyvan.

Taj howled her victory.

Her jubilation only lasted a second.

The craft whipped to the side, and her grip on the craft slipped.

She hung in open air an instant later, the Wyyvan fighter spinning away in front of her.

"Oh...gack," she muttered.

"Hold on!" Dent screamed over the comm.

"To what?" she asked, laughing, finding a sliver of amusement in her situation.

It wasn't the first time she'd been left to gravity's mercy, dangling in the air over Krawlas' surface, but she thought for a second it might be her last.

The dusty ground loomed below her as she flew like a rock.

The fighter she'd taken out toppled end over end a distance in front of her. The pilot dead, it would never recover.

She took solace in that as she followed it, the strings of gravity tugging at her.

Then there was a sharp, brilliant flash as the fighter struck the ground.

Her visor dimmed to save her eyes, which she thought was humorous considering it couldn't do anything to keep her from following the ship down and getting caught up in its explosion.

The flames raced toward her.

Then there was a wall of gray between her and the wreckage.

She slammed hard into something metallic and heard several clangs reverberate through her ears as the impact stunned her.

Her head whirled, and she reached for it to stop the spinning, but she couldn't move. She was trapped.

Taj started to panic, confusion screaming inside her skull. Dent's calm voice came over the comm a moment later.

"I've got you," he told her.

It took her a second to comprehend the words, but the reality of her situation hadn't yet sunk in.

"You've got me?" she asked, having no clue what he meant.

It was only then that she realized she was no longer falling.

She was pinned to the roof of a shuttle, her limbs splayed and stuck to the hull.

"What the…"

"I've engaged the magnetic locks in your suit," the AI explained. "You won't fall, so just hang tight."

As if she had a choice.

"You couldn't have, I don't know, thought to do that earlier?" she asked.

She could almost hear him shrug over the comm.

"Coordination is the cornerstone of good teamwork," he answered. "Had you advised me of your plan to tackle a Wyyvan fighter, I might have been able to devise suitable tactics for such a maneuver. But since you didn't…"

"Gotcha," she replied with a chuckle. "Advise Dent of the crazy stunt before it happens next time. Noted."

There was a flash of light somewhere ahead of her and the shuttles veered off, giving her an unobstructed view of another of their shuttles slamming into the side of one of the Wyyvan fighter craft.

The two went up in a flash.

"Two down," Torbon called out. "Only two more to go."

"*Only*," Cabe growled.

"I was devising a plan to take them out," Dent started, "but our fearless leader decided she needed to hitch a ride, distracting me."

If Taj had been able to shrug, she would have, but the magnetic clasps held her tight. "Sorry," she muttered.

"You almost were," Cabe complained.

"Yell at me later, Cabe," she told him. "What are you thinking, Dent?"

"A moment longer," he answered and went silent.

"Better hurry it up," Lina advised.

She stood on the ground, ineffectively hurling small-arms fire at the two remaining fighters. One of the ships was headed straight toward the shuttle Taj was locked onto.

Taj's scanners picked it up, warning lights flashing across the visor.

"Yeah, I'm with Lina," Taj noted. "I'm not liking being stuck here in the sights of that lizard crawling up my ass."

Bursts of energy streaked past her as the fighter tried to blow her shuttle out of the sky. The shuttle whipped to the side, barely evading the attack. Taj hissed, seeing the energy blasts sear the air not more than a meter away.

"That was too gacking close," she whined. "Dent?"

"Almost done," the AI replied.

"With what?" she asked. She had no clue what he was planning.

"Whatever you're doing, Dent, you better hurry it up," Cabe told him over the comm. "The second fighter is closing."

Taj saw it pop up on her scanner, the other Wyyvan joining the first on her tail.

"Yeah, I agree with Cabe. Hurry!" she said. "Please?" she added.

"There!" Dent shouted. "Got it!"

"Got what?" Taj asked.

She got her answer a second later.

Both fighters dropped into a dive so steep there was no way the move had been natural.

There hadn't even been time for her to catch her breath before the ships hit the ground and exploded, kicking up of clouds of sand and debris and licking flames behind her.

"I hacked their flight systems," Dent explained. "It only works at short distances, but with the shuttle's transmitters to boost the signal, I could gain control of the ships before they could counter my efforts."

"Good timing," Taj told him. "I was starting to get a little airsick up here."

Then the shuttle spun and came in for a landing. The magnetic clamps released as soon as it touched down, and Taj slid off the shuttle's roof and dropped to the ground.

Her legs wobbled beneath her and she nearly fell, only managing to regain her balance at the last second by leaning against the hull.

Cabe was there a second later, wrapping her in a tight embrace.

"Make nice later," Torbon growled as the shuttle's hatch hissed open. "We've got to go." He darted inside, dragging Lina along with him, not giving the engineer time to stop and check on Taj like she wanted to.

"He's right, as much as it pains me to admit it," Dent said, ushering the pair inside just ahead of the hulking form of Krawg. "The Wyyvans held off using the last of their anti-aircraft guns, but they're targeting us with artillery now."

The crew was barely inside when the hatch started to

seal and the shuttle lifted off. They hadn't even reached seats before it was jetting off across the sandy ground, staying low to evade AA fire.

Taj slumped into a seat with a pained sigh.

Krawg dropped into a seat across from her, his helmet sliding back and disappearing into his suit. He had a broad grin plastered across his furry face.

"You are one insane feline," he told her.

She grinned.

"A girl's gotta have a hobby, right?"

"I've repositioned two of our destroyers to keep the Wyyvans from sneaking more of their fighters around the planet," Dent informed them. "I should have thought of it sooner."

"Not like you're built for combat," Lina sympathized.

"Neither are we," Torbon muttered.

"We're learning," Taj shot back.

And they were. It was simply a matter of whether they could stay ahead of the curve. They were battling an army that had experience *and* numbers, as well as just about every other tactical advantage she could think of.

She understood that it would take everything they had to win out here, and time was running out.

"Let's get back to the others," she said. "I need some good, solid dirt beneath my feet for a few minutes so I can think."

CHAPTER SEVEN

After creating a diversion to keep the Wyyvans in the outpost from seeing where the crew departed the shuttle, it dropped them off and returned to where the others were hidden.

The crew rejoined the escaped slaves and returned to the underground network of tunnels they called home.

"This enough solid ground for you?" Torbon asked.

Taj dropped to the hard stone beneath her and smiled up at him, patting the rock. "It'll do."

"That was insane!" Rat exclaimed, staring wide-eyed at Taj. "You're amazing."

"Don't encourage her," Cabe growled at the young female, flopping down beside Taj and grabbing her hand in his. "You scared the gack out of me," he told her.

"Had to fulfill my quota of excitement for the day," she shot back, chuckling.

"You did that, and then some," he said, shaking his head as he pressed his weight against her. "You okay?"

"I hurt like all gack," she admitted, "but I'm all right. Suit's scanners say nothing is broken, but I'm gonna be black and blue under my fur for weeks."

"Better than dead," Lina sniped, coming over and handing Taj a flask of water. Kal and Jadie flanked the engineer, both standing silently, simply listening to the conversation. Harley and Garr walked up a moment later.

Taj took the flask willingly, finishing it in several large gulps.

"Do you always do things like that?" Rat asked, dropping into a squat as she joined the crew.

"Always," Torbon answered.

"Pretty much," Lina said.

"All the gacking time," Cabe assured her, nodding.

"What they said," the Ursite added at the end.

Rat chuckled at the chorus of agreement.

Malcolm and Jak came over and joined them, standing alongside Dent, who'd been silently directing the bots to drop off the supplies they'd sneaked into the tunnels while the crew battled the fighters.

"I don't know whether to pat you on the back or run from you screaming," Jak joked.

"How about neither?" she shot back. "Both would hurt too much right now." She rubbed her temple, groaning at the contact. "My brain feels like it wants to crawl out of my ears and eat my eyes."

"The suit's built-in med systems will kick in shortly," Dent assured her. "It's nothing like the Federation's Pod-docs, but it will suffice for now. Mild painkillers have been injected into your system, and it should be applying soothing and cooling topical anesthetics to your wounds. You should feel it already."

Taj nodded. She'd noticed the pain ebbing as she sat there, but she'd never had the opportunity to test the latest upgrades to Dent's armored suits.

He was always tinkering with them, adding new and better gadgets and changing things. She couldn't keep up with everything, but she was grateful for them all the same —even if Dent had to activate them remotely because Taj didn't have a clue what-all the suit could do.

"I've never seen anything like what you did," Rat gushed, still in awe of what had happened.

"I told you we're here to take our home back," Taj replied. "I'll do whatever is necessary."

"Even if it's stupid and reckless," Cabe added.

"It worked, right?" Taj answered, winking at him.

Cabe sighed, pressing against her tighter. "This time."

"All that matters," she replied.

"But what do we do now?" Torbon asked. "It's only a matter of time before the lizards find a new way to gack with us."

"Stop forcing me to agree with you, Torbon," Dent told him. "I don't like it."

"No one ever does," he shot back, grinning.

"It's clear we can't go straight at them," Cabe added.

"Did you learn anything on your scouting mission?" Jak asked.

Taj shrugged. "I did, but I'm not sure it will be all that helpful at the moment. I was able to pinpoint most of the artillery units and what's left of the AA guns. They're manned by three Wyyvans each, not that it really matters. They're all set up right in the middle of the main thoroughfares, as we've already noted. There's no taking them out without creating way more collateral damage than I'm comfortable with."

"You find where they are keeping the rest of us?" Malcolm asked.

"They're everywhere the soldiers and valuable targets are," she said with a sigh. "The Wyyvans have embedded the hostages anywhere we might hit to keep us from striking those locations."

"Outside of a surgical strike, it appears we would do far more harm to the workers than we would the enemy were we to lash out," Dent announced, reviewing the information Taj had recorded on her trip into the compound.

"So, what do we do?" Rat asked.

Taj wondered about that herself.

She leaned against the stone wall at her back and let her gaze wander, letting her mind drift.

So far, every direct attempt at taking out the Wyyvans had failed. They were too entrenched on the planet to be shaken loose easily. They'd been there too long already and had had too much time to prepare before the Furlorians had come back, which made it hard to picture a scenario that worked to the crew's advantage without someone getting hurt.

Her eyes roamed the rough-hewn ceiling. She wished she had Gran Beaux there to advise her, or Mama Merr to kick her in the ass and inspire her.

Nothing was working out the way she'd imagined it, and she knew that was her lack of experience being reflected back at her.

She'd come to Krawlas with a dream and more hope than sense, and now she was realizing she had too little of both. The dream was becoming a nightmare.

She'd felt so prepared to start, so ready to face the challenge.

Taj knew now how wrong she'd been.

But she had to do something.

If she and the crew packed up and left, there was no way she would ever be able to build another army and come back.

She grunted her frustration. There had to be something they could do; some way of prying the workers from the hands of the Wyyvans so they could blast the outpost to dust.

Then she needed to deal with the enemy fleet.

One thing at a time. She sighed.

A shimmer of metal caught her eye then, and when she glanced across the room at one of the Wyyvan tunneling devices she'd noted earlier, it struck her.

She hopped to her feet, pointing at the machine. "How many of those things do you have?" she asked. "I've seen a couple of them."

Jak followed her gaze. "We stole about ten of them in total, although only eight are operational now."

Taj remembered how quickly the devices had torn into Krawlas' surface, digging massive holes and excavating the precious mineral that had started all this.

"You know how to use them, right?" she asked.

"Got more experience than we care to think about." Malcolm chuckled. "Could run the damn things in my sleep."

Taj grinned. "I think that might be a good thing."

"What you got in mind?" Jak asked, stiffening, wisps of hope playing across his features.

Lina smiled, no doubt realizing what Taj was thinking.

"We could tunnel under the outpost," Taj answered. "Come out near the artillery units, and take the soldiers out, and destroy the weapons while we funnel the remaining workers through the tunnel and back here."

Jak sighed. His shoulders slumped.

"What's wrong?" Taj asked.

"Won't work," Rat answered for the male. "We've tried it a couple times."

"You haven't tried it with us," Torbon said.

"No, but a few extra folks ain't going to make much of a difference," Malcolm stated.

"Why not?" Cabe wondered.

"Like Rat said, we tried it before," Jak went on. "Them lizards figured it out before we got more than a few of our people out and shut us down."

"They set up seismic detectors to warn of unauthorized drilling or tunneling," Malcolm explained. "Since they know where every active tunnel drill site is, they can tell when we're trying to get under them with the machines we stole. They catch us every time we've done it and people die, so we've stopped."

"Not worth the lives," Jak went on. "We made it look like they got the last of us when we tried it months back, but they've still got the systems set up just in case. There's no way around it."

Taj glanced at Dent, an eyebrow raised.

"I presume that eyebrow is asking me whether I can do

anything," he said, offering her a shrug. "The answer is, 'I don't know.' While I was hacking the flight systems of the fighters, I scanned the surrounding area for other systems I might grab control of..."

"And?" Lina asked.

"This is where the bad news comes in," Krawg jumped in, "or Dent would have started rambling technical mumbo-jumbo none of us understand rather than pausing dramatically."

"I did not 'pause dramatically,' I simply paused," Dent defended himself. "But he's correct, nevertheless. The systems on this planet are as basic as they come. The Wyyvans, either because of our earlier presumption that they don't want to draw attention or because they simply don't have access to better equipment, have implemented an almost purely mechanical arrangement to gather the Toradium-42 ore."

"So there's nothing to hack into?" Lina asked.

Dent shook his head. "I can possibly circumvent the automated vehicles, but I detected little else that might aid us."

"Could we run the vehicles into the guns?" Cabe asked.

"They're hardly substantial enough to do damage, even when they are loaded," Dent replied.

"The locations of the weapons makes that a bad idea," Taj added. "We'd hurt people if we did that, which is what we're trying to avoid."

"I hate to be 'that guy,' but maybe we need to rethink what we're willing to do here," Kal said with a shrug. "I don't want to hurt anyone, of course, but—"

"But nothing," Rat growled. "Those are our people in there."

Kal raised his hands in surrender. "I'm simply throwing out ideas and seeing what sticks," he replied.

"I've got someplace to stick your idea," Rat warned.

Krawg chuckled. "I like this kid."

"We're not looking to hurt anyone," Taj assured the young female, then turned her attention to Jak and Malcolm. "I do have an idea, but we'll need your help."

"If it gets our people out safely, you've got it," Jak told her.

"That's the plan." Taj nodded. "You think you can get more of the drilling machines?"

"Yeah," Jak answered, eyes narrowing. "Since you showed up and the Wyyvans pulled back to the outpost, the machines are sitting around undefended. But I already told you the lizards can detect and pinpoint seismic disturbances."

Taj grinned. "I'm counting on it."

Taj and the crew crouched a short distance outside the outpost, having sneaked back under cover of the growing darkness.

"We ready to do this?" Taj asked.

"I am if you are," Dent replied.

"Then hit it," she ordered.

"Literally," Torbon added with a grin.

Seconds later, brilliant flashes of energy illuminated the sky. It looked like lightning, even though Taj knew it wasn't.

There was a sharp crack of thunder and a section of the wall exploded, then another was blasted a moment later.

Alarms sounded in the compound, and the crew stared at the outpost as yet another blast struck the opposite side, then another to the west of that.

"Is everyone in place?" Taj asked over the comm.

"Waiting on the order," Jadie came back.

"Ready here," Kal added a moment later.

Harley and Garr offered their affirmations right after, the crew having given them communicators so they could stay in touch.

"Hold," Taj shot back, turning to look at Dent.

"If the Wyyvans aren't already at their posts, they will be shortly," the AI said. "I'd suggest giving them a few more seconds, then moving ahead with the plan."

Taj nodded and glanced at the outpost walls, where the *Decimator* had pinpointed and taken out several of the artillery units that had been installed.

There'd been a risk of hurting the workers, but Taj had made sure that Dent only targeted those units away from the population centers and with the lowest chance of screwing up and creating collateral damage.

She could see soldiers scrambling across the wall, staring out into the coming night, trying to find the attack they were expecting to follow on the heels of the ship's fire.

It wouldn't come the way they imagined.

"Do it," she ordered.

In the distance, out on the Maladorian Plains, an explosion sounded, vibrating through the ground. A second one followed right after, then a third and a fourth and a fifth went off, each one ten seconds after the last.

Dent stiffened, and although Taj wanted to nag him, she waited impatiently for him to speak. It wasn't until the tenth explosion sounded that he nodded to her.

Artillery fire leapt into the air then, flares of energy streaking toward where the explosions had gone off.

"Their response time is impressive," Krawg noted.

She had expected exactly that. The Wyyvans were hitting back at the locations where the explosions had occurred, clued into the exact coordinates by the seismic devices the Wyyvans used to determine when the rebel slaves were attempting to use the stolen tunneling devices.

"You get what you needed?" Taj asked.

"I did," the AI answered.

She grinned and activated her comm. "Keep them distracted a little longer," she said over the link.

"Will do," Jadie replied. "This is fun."

"Leave it to your aunt to enjoy playing with explosives," Cabe told Torbon.

Torbon shrugged. "Who doesn't like things that go boom?"

Taj grinned.

He had a point.

CHAPTER EIGHT

Back in the rebel tunnels, Taj met with Jak as his people flitted about, organizing the influx of new supplies and getting ready to follow up on Taj's plan of action.

"Things go okay?" she asked.

He nodded. "We managed to grab ten more of the tunneling devices while you distracted the Wyyvans. We're moving the machines into place now," he said. "I'm still not sure this is going to work, though."

"As long as we pull our end off, it'll work fine," Taj told him. "Dent managed to pinpoint where the seismic devices are located by tracing the surge of power after every explosion."

Jak whistled. "He'd have to be damn sensitive to pick out something that minute."

"While the devices aren't on a computer system, offering me a direct line to them, their nature makes it easy to determine their location," Dent explained. "The entire electrical system of the outpost is automated, the lights and vehicles and other equipment uniformly on or off. Thus, they maintain a relatively steady level of energy output. The seismic devices, however, spike every time they detect an unauthorized vibration in the area as they are set to read and record the movement. With the timed explosions as a control factor, I was able to figure out where in the system the spikes occurred."

"And in true Wyyvan fashion, all the devices are located in the exact same place, making our job even easier," Taj finished, chuckling. "Military efficiency at its dumbest."

"Well, in their defense," Dent stated, "their escaped captives don't have access to high-tech equipment to do refined searches like this."

"Gack, the Wyyvans don't even *have* high-tech equip-ment," Torbon said.

"My point exactly," Dent went on. "They weren't prepared for anyone to track down their devices, so why bother spreading them out?"

"Common sense?" Taj said. "Logic? Just plain, good gacking tactical reasoning?"

"Since when have the Wyyvans shown any of those traits?" Cabe asked.

"It's a good thing they haven't," Lina said. "We've got enough problems with the numbers and circumstances. The last thing we need is a smart enemy."

"Are you sure you can take these devices out?" Jak asked, clearly still unsure of the crew's capabilities.

Taj understood his reluctance.

He'd made it clear that he didn't want to put his people at more of a risk than necessary, but Taj and her people kept poking at the enemy and riling them up. Sooner or later they were going to lash out in a big way, and there was a good chance that Jak's people would be caught in the crossfire.

That was why they needed to hurry.

"We'll take them out," she assured him. "We just need your people to be in position and ready to pull off the next phase of the plan."

"Can't say I like it much, seeing how many people we've lost trying similar plans, but we're trusting you and your crew. I hope that trust isn't misplaced."

"We appreciate the passive-aggressive support," Torbon sniped, shaking his head.

Jak turned on him. "Look, we don't know you any more than you know us, boy," he fired back. "We were doing fine before you arrived, and now my people are in danger again because of you." He jabbed a finger in Torbon's direction.

"That's right, you were doing so well," Torbon replied. "All that food and water you were sitting on and all those opportunities you just hadn't tapped yet." He let out a bark of laughter. "I hate to say it, but you were biding your time, waiting to die. It wouldn't have been much longer before you would have been forced to move on and abandon your people if you wanted to have any chance of surviving. Most likely, all of you would have died out in the desert.

"At least now you have a fighting chance—a real opportunity to see your friends freed of the Wyyvans. A chance to reunite your families that you didn't have before we arrived."

Jak growled, "What the hell do you know about what we're going through?"

Torbon chuckled and glanced at Jadie before looking back at Jak. "I know exactly what you're feeling. We were there not too long ago," he admitted. "These lizard gacks don't give a damn about anyone but themselves, and mostly not even that. We got to spend a lot of time up close and personal with a couple of them."

He gestured in the general direction of the outpost.

"Maybe not today, or even tomorrow, but before you know it, as soon as the lizards are done doing what they want to do here, every single one of you is going to be killed by them. Slaughtered because you no longer serve a purpose and they don't want to be bothered by you."

"Still sounds like you're talking out your ass, Boy," Jak said. "Guessing."

Torbon stepped into his face.

"The gacksacks held our people hostage; held my aunt captive," he went on. "The only way to deal with them is to kill them before they kill you."

Taj stuck a hand between the two and separated them.

"He's right, and I don't even mind saying it this time," she announced.

"What has the world come to?" Krawg sighed. "That's like...what, three times or something today? Must be a record. Someone needs to write this down."

"Maybe you *do* know what we're going through," Malcolm said, "but you're putting our people's lives at risk with a plan we can't be sure will even work."

"We're also putting our own lives at risk," Taj countered. "We'll be the ones who attack the Wyyvan soldiers, to be the ones to enter the outpost and go after the devices."

"We could just as easily pack up and leave," Cabe added.

"Besides, some of those people in there are ours, too," Lina reminded everyone. "There are Furlorians we mistakenly left behind suffering right alongside your people. We're not taking any of these decisions lightly, I assure you. If we gack up, we lose right along with you."

Jak sighed, his glare evaporating into a look of weary resignation. He nodded.

Taj realized that the male was conflicted, trying to walk the fence while staying strong in front of his people.

"Just be sure not to start working before we give the order," Taj clarified. "The seismic devices need to be out of commission or the Wyyvans will put their all into taking them out. Then any chance we have a trying this in the future is gone."

"You don't need to explain the consequences," Malcolm snapped.

"We understand," Jak said, caught between Malcolm's fury and the realization that there was little hope to be had if the plan didn't work.

It wasn't just the Furlorians' time that was running out, it was everyone's.

After an awkward silence, the crew said their goodbyes and left the rebels' tunnels.

"You sure about this?" Lina asked once they'd reached the outpost.

"You know how I feel about that question," Taj growled.

The engineer shrugged. "Doesn't make it any less valid a question," she replied with a sly grin.

"As seems to be our lot of late, we're running out of options," Taj answered, raising her hands in frustration. "If this doesn't work, we're likely looking at retreating. I don't want to do that."

"The Wyyvans will lock this place down tight if we do," Cabe argued. "We won't get another shot at taking Krawlas back *or* getting our people out of here."

Like Malcolm, Taj didn't need to be told the consequences of failure. She knew gacking well what would happen if they couldn't negate the seismic devices and get the workers out from under Wyyvan control.

She'd watched as Captain Vort executed friends and family, and the Wyyvan grand admiral was a pettier, more sadistic lizard than Vort could ever be.

Taj could deal with losing Krawlas again—although it would hurt—but she couldn't forgive herself for leaving her people behind, even if she hadn't known she had.

That was something that needed to be rectified, no matter what.

They needed to be free again, and Taj was willing to kill to make that happen.

She was willing to die, too, if necessary.

But she'd definitely rather kill, if she were honest with herself.

Taj chuckled at the thought, and the crew glanced at her, giving her strange looks for her sudden outburst. She shrugged, blowing it off.

"We can't make it obvious we're going after the seismic devices," Taj explained, "so we need to make a bit of a mess in other areas and delay them finding out we're hitting the machines for as long as possible."

"I can make quite a mess," Torbon assured her, grinning broadly.

"No argument here," Lina muttered.

"I've been known to cause a bit of chaos now and again," Krawg added.

"Mostly with the funk that wafts off his fur," Torbon joked.

The hulking Ursite snarled at Torbon. "I can start the chaos off by shooting a certain cat."

"I'm tempted to let you do it," Taj told him, "but we need him right now. Maybe later?"

"I look forward to it," Krawg answered, turning his toothy grin on Torbon.

"Nice of you to make plans for me, Taj," Torbon complained.

"Don't worry," Lina told him, "I won't let them kill you too badly." She patted him on the arm.

"I feel better already." He grunted, shaking his head.

"Let's get this gackshow on the road," Taj said.

As they'd planned, the crew separated, each member going to a different area of the outpost to wreak havoc. Taj and Dent stuck together, but Torbon, Lina, Krawg, and Cabe split up and made their way around the outpost to enter at different points.

Taj hated that everyone was going in on their own, but it was better to make a stealthy entry than form up and hit the Wyyvans hard.

Their efforts were more to unbalance the enemy; throw them off and confuse them rather than take out any significant number of the soldiers. There wasn't much hope for a body count, and trying to pile one up would only make things worse for the workers stuck inside the outpost.

The Wyyvans had already determined that Taj and her

people wanted to minimize collateral damage, so it only made sense that the next step in the Wyyvan tactical march would be to start using the workers as hostages against the Furlorians.

Taj wanted to get in and out before they made that choice. It was one thing to have them passively use the workers as shields, but it was something else entirely if the Wyyvans started actively leveraging the workers' lives against Taj and her crew.

She and Dent clambered up the wall after watching the guards for a few minutes, making sure they could get in unseen.

The Wyyvans had upped security, but it was still pathetic given how low-tech their equipment was. Dent's buried device continued to block transmissions from the outpost to the Wyyvan fleet, and with no spacecraft on the planet itself, there was nothing the lizards could do to detect the tiny trace movements of the sneaking crew.

And no matter how important the guards' jobs were in theory, no matter what the species, it was almost a certainty that the guards would do a gack-poor job. It was simply too boring a task to stay alert for very long.

Sure enough, the guards made a show of working hard while hardly working.

Taj and Dent slipped inside with ease, and the others reported that they, too, had gotten into the mining complex without problems.

She wondered maybe if it had been *too* easy, but she could see the efforts of the soldiery as they went about their tasks. They were trying, however ineffectually, to protect the grand admiral's investment on the planet, but it was clear that Galforin had been guiding the project from above.

Now that he had been cut off from his soldiers, there was a clear lack of organization above and beyond the day-to-day norm. The head had been cut off, and the limbs had begun to wither.

Taj grinned at the lesson she'd learned from Vort and his soldiers, especially from the blind Wyyvan, S'thlor, who they'd left on Corzant.

The Wyyvan leaders didn't trust the soldiers, and the soldiers didn't trust the leaders.

Their entire system was built upon fear and consequences, not discipline or respect. When the soldiers were left to their own devices, they practically shut down out of fear of doing something that might come back to bite them in the tail.

They did what they were told to do and avoided over-thinking anything.

Well, they avoided *thinking* about anything, let alone overthinking. It simply wasn't safe to be independent or an individual.

And that was how the Wyyvans in the outpost were going about their tasks: by rote. They were doing what had been drilled into them and nothing more.

So when the explosions started erupting across the outpost, the expected chaos broke loose.

Cabe struck the northeastern corner, targeting one of the artillery units, and Lina and Torbon and Krawg had chosen random sections of the outpost to do the same.

The crew had rigged small explosive devices made of the Toradium-42 that was abundant all over the planet.

The rebels had a small stash of it in the abandoned mining tunnels they'd made their home in, so it was easy to create small bombs.

While the mineral was surprisingly stable, Dent had determined how best to trigger the release of its energy and harness it explosively. That had been what they'd used to blast the desert and set off the seismic devices.

With it being so plentiful, it only made sense to take advantage of it.

The irony of using it to take out Wyyvans, considering that Toradium-42 was what had started all this, wasn't lost on Taj.

It made the idea far more appealing.

She and Dent made their way through the outpost's streets, dodging the automated vehicles and the soldiers darting about, doing their best to cope with what was going on.

It wasn't long before they reached the small building that contained the seismic devices and the small group of soldiers stationed there to protect and operate them.

Two Wyyvan guards stood outside, clearly grateful to have a defined purpose. Their masks filtered moisture and bubbled with every breath as Taj and Dent surveyed the scene, the two having circled around opposite sides of the building.

The nearby streets were clear of soldiers, the majority of them running around attempting to bolster the defenses at the artillery units, so Taj and Dent barely bothered with subterfuge.

Taj stepped around the corner and dashed at the guard.

He spun around, eyes wide behind his visor, and Taj drove her blade into his chest, twisting it for maximum effect.

The second guard went for his gun.

He never got his hands on it.

Dent came up behind him and snapped the lizard's neck with a *pop*. The Wyyvan went stiff and dropped without a sound.

They'd decided ahead of time who would go through the door first, so Taj put her boot into it and kicked it open, rushing inside. Dent took a few seconds to collect the corpses of the two Wyyvan guards and drag them inside before shutting the door behind him.

Two more obvious guards stood just inside the room, guns in their hands, while three more Wyyvans stood around looking surprised as Dent dropped bodies on the floor.

Taj stepped in, swinging her blade to the left and nearly hacking off the head of the Wyyvan she hit. He stumbled back, clutching his throat as black blood spewed between his fingers.

Taj shot him then and turned the gun on the second guard. He'd managed to raise his weapon and go for the trigger, but Taj was faster. She double-tapped him in the chest, then popped him once in the head for good measure.

Dent stepped around her and shot the other three Wyyvans in turn, only the last of the group managing to cry out before he died.

Given the noise outside, Cabe and the others still tossing bombs at the artillery units, Taj was sure no one had heard him.

Before he hit the ground, Taj began dissecting the seismic machines.

She put her blade to work, slicing and chopping and slashing at the delicate electronics, carving each into tiny pieces that could never be reassembled no matter how much effort the Wyyvans put into it.

Taj had worried that they might have spare devices, so Dent searched the room, finding one and a number of spare parts. He destroyed those quickly, and the pair returned to the door after making certain they'd left nothing behind.

"You think we got them all?" Taj asked.

Dent shrugged. "We can't know if they have others elsewhere, but it's not likely they do," he answered. "We don't have time to worry about it, regardless. We need to—"

The AI stiffened, eyes going wide.

"What is it?" she asked.

"The Gate is being accessed!"

CHAPTER NINE

"Gack it!" Taj growled as they slipped out of the seismic device room, having wedged the door shut behind them.

It would delay anyone determined to get inside, but Taj figured that if no one looked closely at the place or thought about it, they'd bought themselves a little more time to pull off her plan.

The arrival of Wyyvan reinforcements, however, hadn't been part of that plan even though she had known it was a possibility.

Should have tried to take that damn Gate out to start with, Taj thought, snarling at herself for not having thought of it.

She had a long way to go before she become a true tactician.

Dent spent the race back to the tunnels tuned into the armada, registering what was being passed on to him. It wasn't until after they'd made it inside the cavernous main room of the rebel headquarters that he seemed ready to reveal what was happening.

Jak looked at them worriedly as they arrived. "Did you get them all?" he asked.

"We did, but we've got bigger problems now," Taj told him.

He groaned and ran a hand across his brow. "Such as?"

"Troop carriers are breaking through the Gate the Wyyvans opened above," Dent explained. "Four of them have emerged so far, but sensors detect a half-dozen more preparing to come through."

Taj slumped at hearing the specifics. "That has to be thousands of soldiers," she said.

Dent didn't confirm her assumption.

He also didn't contradict it, she noticed.

"There is no way we can repel that many soldiers," Malcolm spat. "We can't even take out the ones who are here already."

Taj agreed.

"Sic the armada on them, Dent," she ordered. "We can't let them get anywhere near the planet or we're gacked!"

"Already on it," he confirmed, "but the bulk of the enemy fleet is already advancing, pushing forward at a fast clip toward Krawlas."

"At least it can't get any worse," Torbon stated as he and the others joined them.

Everyone groaned.

"Did you really just say that?" Taj asked. "Why didn't you just ask Rowl to swat us down while you're at it?"

"Uh…" Dent started, glancing at Torbon, then back at Taj. "Your god is feeling cruel today," he said. "The advance of the Wyyvan fleet toward the planet has weakened my efforts to block their transmissions, and they've broken through. I'm picking up encrypted communications between the dreadnought and the outpost's command unit."

"*Now* it can't get any worse," Torbon said, smiling. "Right?"

"Bloody Rowl!" Taj muttered. "I hate you, Torbon. Stop cursing us!" She sighed, turning back to the AI. "What are they saying, Dent?"

"Grand Admiral Galforin has ordered a sweep of the area surrounding the outpost," Dent answered. "Scorched ground. His forces will be pushing out almost in their entirety in a few moments."

Taj growled and turned to face Jak. "Now would be a good time to get your people working," she told him. "Might want to light a fire under their asses while you're at it."

Malcolm snarled and ran off, darting down a nearby tunnel.

The artillery fire shrieked in the distance and the ground rumbled at the impacts, motes of dust dancing down from the ceiling.

"They won't find us anytime soon," Jak said, clearly trying to sound more hopeful than his expression showed.

"Anytime is too soon," Rat mumbled.

"Might be sooner than you think," Cabe suggested. "They have to know we're hiding somewhere underground." He stared at the rocky ceiling. "And since they've had seismic devices to be sure you weren't digging additional holes, it won't take a huge leap of logic for them to start targeting old dig sites since you couldn't have made many new holes out here."

Jak stiffened. He apparently hadn't thought of that until then.

"Judging by the way the landscape looks, that's still a lot of places to cover," Taj said, trying to reassure everyone.

"Way fewer than if they're just taking random shots into the Plains," he countered.

"A systematic sweep of the already-mined areas will bring them to us far quicker than is good for us," Dent agreed.

"Wyyvan troops are spilling from the outpost," Jadie reported. She'd gone with Kal and set up a watch while Taj and the others assaulted the devices. "There are a gacking lot of them." Her voice quavered, even over the comm.

Taj stood there for a moment running scenarios through her head, wishing she had more experience to rely on. What she'd learned from Beaux was mostly how to slip away and hide, and how to avoid major confrontations to keep their people alive.

That had been the way of the Furlorians since Felinus 4.

That, however, wasn't an option here.

"We need to step up the fight, then," she decided, knowing she'd regret the words later. This wasn't a situation where running away or spending time deliberating made any sense, though.

It was time to fight.

"We don't exactly have an army," Cabe offered, not looking all that excited by the prospect of taking on the Wyyvans directly.

"No, we don't," she replied, "but we have air support."

"Which also happens to be our way off this planet," Krawg argued. "We'd be sending them into a meat grinder with so many of those artillery units still in place."

"He's correct," Dent stated. "The odds of our shuttles surviving are—"

Krawg shook his head, interrupting with a cough. "Never tell me the odds."

Torbon chuckled. "That'd make a good line in a holovid. Someone should write that down."

"Along with our eulogy?" Lina asked. "Hate being negative, but we're risking an awful lot here. Between the enemy fleet closing in on our ships and the chance of our shuttles being destroyed, do you think this is a good move?"

Taj met the engineer's gaze and tried to smile. "We only have a few choices, Lina," she argued. She held up a finger. "We grab everyone, load them into the shuttles, and return to the armada, hoping we can get away without being wiped out." Another finger rose. "We can pack into the shuttles and flee in them, not bothering with the *Decimator* and the other ships." She lifted a third finger. "Or we can fight." Taj lowered the first two fingers. "I vote for the last of the three."

"I *so* don't want to agree with you on this particular subject, but I'd rather go out fighting for our world than dying while trying to run away with my tail tucked between my legs," Cabe said.

Torbon nodded. "Me too," he agreed with a resigned sigh.

"We can always vote for number three until a fourth option arrives," Krawg suggested.

"The *Decimator* reports that the battle is fierce," Dent said. "Our ships are giving as good as they are receiving, but it's a game of attrition at this point. We won't win the numbers game."

"Gacking Rowl!" Taj snarled. "Leave enough shuttles in reserve to get all of us out of here and send the rest after the ground troops," she ordered. "I don't have to ask you to try not to get them all blown to gack, do I?"

Dent chuckled. "No, that goes without saying."

"Except that she said it," Torbon muttered. "And you guys say *I* make no sense."

The cavern trembled as the artillery barrage moved closer.

Jak grunted. "I'll get everyone ready."

Taj shook her head. "No, you and your people stay here," she told him.

His eyes narrowed in confusion. "And have the roof come down on us?"

"That's why we're going out," Taj explained. "We're going to draw their fire and keep them from getting to you and your people."

Jak stared at her, head cocked to the side. "I don't understand. Why would you do this?"

"Two reasons," she answered. "The first is, we need your people to keep digging. We still want to get everyone out of the outpost if we can. The second reason is that our arrival brought this down on you. If we go out in a blaze of glory, Rowl forbid, and your people stay out of sight and out of the way, maybe things can go back to the way they were. Maybe you'll have a chance."

Jak continued to stare without saying anything.

"If nothing else, you can commandeer the remaining shuttles and make a break for it."

Dent nodded. "I've set the access to allow you to board and take control of the shuttles should we perish."

"I don't know what to say," Jak replied.

"Don't say anything," Taj answered. "Just get as many of your people out of here alive as you can if things go badly." She glanced at Rat.

Rat waggled a finger her direction. "Don't go looking at me, now," she said. "I'm going with you." She raised her rifle, grinning.

There wasn't time to argue, so Taj nodded her reluctant approval and spun on a heel, racing off. She knew her crew would follow.

They had to get out of the tunnels and make a big enough show of force to draw as much of the Wyyvan force to them as possible if there was to be any chance of keeping the escaped workers safe.

She exited the tunnels just as the shuttles engaged the Wyyvan soldiers in the distance. Explosions filled the air, the screech of energy weapons drowning out almost everything else. The ships darted back and forth, strafing the ground and doing their best to avoid being shot down.

Taj saw one get blown away not more than a few seconds after the first engagement. It didn't bode well, but there was nothing she could do about it from there. They had to get moving.

The crew turned on their camo programs and surrounded Rat so she'd benefit from the distortion as they traveled.

Taj regretted that they didn't have an extra suit of

armor for the girl, but she decided to stick close to her and make sure she didn't get hurt. She didn't need any more deaths on her conscience.

As quickly as they could, they made their way around the flank of the main push of soldiers. The entire time, she cringed as the artillery moved closer and closer to the rebel tunnels, but before it could reach them, Taj ordered her people to scatter and open up on the troops to draw them off.

"Let's do this!"

Her people leapt up and unleashed a barrage of fire on the Wyyvans. The shuttles continued their assault, weaving in and out of the falling rain of artillery fire. It amazed her at how well Dent could multitask.

She glanced at him, and he didn't seem the slightest bit fazed by the effort of commanding an armada in a pitched battle in space and a shuttle war down here, and now he had added a fevered gunfight to the mess.

"How's the *Decimator* doing?" she asked, although she wasn't entirely sure she wanted to know.

"Holding its own," he answered, "but the Wyyvan troop carriers are almost all free of the Gate. They're trailing behind the main fleet."

Taj cursed under her breath.

"The two destroyers still protecting the Gate?"

He ducked a blaster bolt and returned fire, killing the Wyyvan who had shot at him. "One joined the rest of the fleet to bolster its numbers. Galforin is holding the carriers back to ensure they aren't taken out, plus he's keeping his command ship out of the fight. Either we damaged it worse than we thought earlier, or he simply doesn't want to put himself at risk."

"Probably the last," Taj stated, knowing how cowardly Wyyvan commanders were, having seen it firsthand.

She spent the next several minutes battling it out with the Wyyvan soldiers at range. The shuttles backed them up, decimating the ranks far better than the small-arms fire the Furlorians were throwing at them.

Taj cringed as one of her people was struck by multiple blasts at once. Bel was her name. It popped to mind as she died, and Taj growled low in her throat at the loss. Then another Furlorian died, then another, and for the life of her, Taj couldn't think of their names right then, her people's identity hidden behind the armored visors.

"Gack!" Lina howled, spraying the enemy with her automatic energy rifle.

Taj squeezed off shot after shot as the enemy continued to advance, their black armor making the troops look as though there was an army of insects crawling toward the crew.

"Hate to ask this right now, but is this the whole plan?" Cabe inquired, moving up alongside Taj as he lashed out at the encroaching enemy.

It kind of was...

Then she decided it couldn't be.

"Gack, no!" she shouted in defiance.

She'd been emotionally ready to go out in a blaze of glory and do everything she had to do to stop the Wyyvans from finding and killing the rebels, but that was being defeatist, she realized.

Taj glanced at Rat, watched her for a moment, thrilling

at the girl's ferocity and willingness to fight for a cause she believed in.

Taj couldn't let her down. She couldn't let her people down, either.

She wouldn't let *anyone* down.

"I have an idea!" she cried out.

"Oh…gack!" Lina muttered. "Duck and cover, folks!"

CHAPTER TEN

G rand Admiral Galforin slammed his fist on the console in front of his seat.

"Crush them!" he growled. "I want these rodents dead!"

XO Volg called out from his station, "Those creatures are resilient, Admiral. As much as I want to comply with your orders, we are losing troops nearly one for one in the fight, sir. We can't maintain this pace if we wish to retain the fleet at fighting strength without joining the fight ourselves."

Galforin shook his head. "I won't martyr myself to save a few ships, Volg."

"Of course not," Volg replied.

Despite his determination to win, he didn't dare risk the *Stormfront*. Too much was at stake, and if he lost the dreadnought, his power at home would be nothing, regardless of how much of the Toradium-42 he returned with. The *Stormfront* was the symbol of his power and control over his forces. To lose it would mean losing everything, and the cowardly sneak attack by the unknown enemy force had already wrought enough damage on the ship.

"Our ground forces," he asked, shifting gears before being forced to make a decision. "How do they fare?"

XO Volg took a moment to examine the reports. He looked up with a sly grin on his broad lips. "It would appear that the invading force might more accurately be called a farce, Admiral."

Galforin spun in his seat to face the XO. "What do you mean, Volg?"

"Although the transmission hack is still wreaking havoc, causing sporadic outages in our communications, the current sitrep is that the invaders have crawled out of their holes to meet our soldiers in the open. There appear to be less than forty of them, Admiral."

"Forty?" Grand Admiral Galforin leapt out of his seat, stomping over to where Volg sat. "That can't be true."

"See for yourself," Volg offered, motioning to the console. The data flowed across it, and Volg highlighted the pertinent information to make it easier for the admiral to examine.

"Most of the damage is being inflicted by their shuttles, which are automated if my readings are correct," XO Volg explained.

"We're being assaulted by a cluster of pirates and bots?" Galforin shouted.

"It would appear so, sir," Volg replied, fingers tapping on the screen in hopes of getting further information.

"How is this even possible?" Galforin asked.

"I believe they have an AI at their disposal. It's coordinating the attack on at least two fronts if the signals we've intercepted are to be believed."

"Can you block it?" the admiral asked. "Shut it down?"

Volg shook his head. "The encryption is too advanced. We don't have the time or tools to even attempt it," he admitted. "We're able to see the transmission because the source isn't bothering to hide it. It's completely confident of its abilities."

"For good reason, it seems." Galforin groaned. "Is there nothing that can be done to counter its control?"

"I don't believe that would be the route to take," the XO advised.

"Tell me then, Volg, what would *you* do if you were in charge?"

Galforin bit back a grin. The question was loaded, and he wanted to see how Volg handled it.

"I would, of course, defer to you, Admiral, since I would not be in a position of superiority over you," the XO stated without hesitation, deftly avoiding the trap. "I would simply advise you to focus on the aspect of the battle most likely to be won."

"And that would be?"

"The fight on the planet, sir," Volg told him. "Release more of the Vipers, punish these invaders, and remove their most effective weapons: the shuttle fleet protecting them from above."

Volg brought up a hazy map that showed the most recent placements of both the enemy and the admiral's troops. The XO trailed a finger across it.

"Here we have their ground forces," he explained. "As you can see, they are hardly a threat in numbers, although they definitely have the advantage in ferocity. But that can be turned if we cull their air support. A full contingent of Vipers would eliminate their aerial superiority."

"Forcing them to retreat on the planet or back to their fleet," Galforin finish, grinning all the while.

Volg nodded. "As of now, their ships all appear to be automated, just as their shuttles are. They have no flesh in the fight, so they can afford to trade losses with us. There is no collateral damage connected to it."

Galforin turned around and glanced at the large view screen in front of his station. He surveyed the enemy fleet as the battle went on, seeing the attrition wearing at his forces.

His soldiers would break. Of that, he was certain.

It was simply a matter of when.

Could he hold them together long enough to win? That was the question.

Volg was right, he realized. There was little chance to win the battle in space while maintaining the morale and composure of his soldiers, but he *could* win the fight below and turn the tide in his favor.

"Release the Vipers," he ordered. "All of them. I want those rodents torn apart."

Volg relayed the order, eyes on his screen the entire time, awaiting a response. He called a moment later, "Vipers away."

Galforin nodded and returned to his station, dropping into his seat.

"What of the ships they dispatched to block their path?" the admiral asked.

"We'll lose a few, Admiral," Volg answered, "but it won't

impact their effectiveness. Those two destroyers are too slow to contain our fighters or do much more than harangue them for a short distance."

The admiral tapped his fingers on the arm of his chair, pleased, eyes locked on the screen as he watched the battle play out.

As much as he believed the XO's advice would sway the fight his way, he had other concerns.

For whatever reason, the enemy fleet had chosen not to fire directly upon the mining compound on KI1047-32. He didn't know if it was weakness or simply a blessing to be grateful for, but the enemy's response to his decision to retreat at the first confrontation had been telling.

Still, there was a chance that the enemy would become desperate when they realized the fight was shifting against them, and Galforin needed to protect his investment.

"Bring us into play subtly," he ordered his XO. "Maintain distance, but place us where we can intervene should the enemy decide they want to take punitive measures upon the compound before they fall."

Galforin could feel Volg's eyes on his back.

"Sir?" the XO asked.

"You heard me, Volg," he told the commander. "We can remain outside the engagement and at the edge of safe distance from the planet, but we cannot let them destroy all the work we've accomplished below. I won't allow it."

"Yes, sir," Volg replied after a second's hesitation.

Galforin knew the male would do what he was told, but he understood the XO's hesitation. To get too near the planet with an alien force above was to flirt with death a bit too boldly for either of their tastes.

But in life, all rewards must be weighed against the risks. In this case, Grand Admiral Galforin believed the reward far outweighed the danger he exposed them to.

Regardless, his hands trembled as the XO followed his directive, but he hid them to keep anyone from noticing.

Galforin could give in to his nerves once the enemy was vanquished, not before.

CHAPTER ELEVEN

"We've got incoming," Dent called.

Taj followed his eyes to the sky and growled low in her throat. Although they were currently little more than black specks against the pale blue horizon, she knew what was coming.

"Gack it all!" she snarled.

She looked at her people spread out across the field and realized how little protection that distance offered against the mass of Wyyvan fighters screaming their way.

She was glad she'd relayed her orders before they'd arrived, or any chance they had of survival would be nil—not that even perfect execution of her plan offered much hope of better odds. But at least the handful of shuttles she'd sent the back ranks had peeled off before they could be shot down.

"How's the loading going?" she asked Dent.

He paused for only an instant before replying, and Taj knew he'd been communicating with the bots. "The first two shuttles are loaded and away. A third is almost ready, and the others are in process. Won't be much longer before they are airborne."

Taj groaned, despite knowing her complaints would do nothing to speed things up. "We're gonna need one right away."

Dent didn't even bother to reply.

"Spread out, people!" Cabe shouted over the comm. "Make it as hard as possible for these approaching fighters to target you."

"We could always jump on their backs like Taj did," Torbon laughed.

"Yeah, because that worked out so well, huh?" Taj asked, recalling how she'd only made it through because of Dent and the shuttle he'd summoned to keep her from becoming a bloody splat on the ravaged terrain.

A few moments later, the Vipers joined the fight. They streaked across the sky and engaged the shuttles without mercy.

Two of the shuttles evaporated in fierce explosions as soon as the Wyyvan fighters made contact.

Dent adjusted then, disengaging them from the ground troops and turning their focus to the fighters. The Wyyvan soldiers pushed forward as soon as the pressure was off.

Taj ducked and darted to the left, dodging the sudden burst of renewed fire that came in their direction. Another of the Furlorians fell, and Rat just managed to slip away from an energy burst that nearly took her head off.

"Stay low, girl," Taj growled at Rat, despite feeling like a hypocrite.

There were Furlorians as young as Rat in the battle, and several of them had died already.

The only grace Taj could retain regarding the situation was that the Furlorians had come to the planet of their own accord. Sure, they'd followed her, but they had had a choice to come and fight for the planet of their birth.

Rat didn't have that option.

She'd been dragged to the planet and enslaved, forced to work for masters who didn't care for her on a planet where she didn't belong.

For Taj to see Rat die for such an empty cause would be far too bitter a bite of cruel fate for her to take.

Two more Furlorians fell under the barrage and Taj growled, wanting to look away but needing to record their deaths in her mind.

These people can't be forgotten.

She returned fire, taking out five Wyyvans in trade for the two Furlorian lives, but there was little satisfaction in it.

The enemy outnumbered them still, and there was no doubt the tide was turning against them. It wouldn't be long until all her people had fallen, and then the whole effort would have been for nothing.

Taj battled on, unwilling to quit despite her guilt, then heard a wild whoop at her back. She cast a furtive glance over her shoulder to see Rat grinning and hollering.

Behind her came the rebels, bolting across the scrubland, weapons raised and firing.

"I knew they wouldn't let us down!" Rat cried out.

Taj hoped she was right.

Jak and Malcolm formed up alongside the Furlorians

and crew and launched a furious barrage of fire toward the Wyyvans. The enemy lines slowed in response, their advance grinding to a stop under the assault of the rebels' bolt rifles.

Taj smiled at the familiar sound she hadn't heard arriving on Corzant. It was strangely comforting.

She glanced at Jak as he came up beside her. "I hope you didn't bring everyone," she told him.

"Everyone we could spare," he answered, jerking his chin over his shoulder with a laugh. "Got an eighty-five-year-old grandpa in the pile somewhere, lobbing bolts at the enemy."

Taj grinned at that, picturing the old male because she couldn't see him.

At least if he was going to die today, he'd go out on his terms—like a warrior.

Still, Taj felt she had to warn Jak about what he was getting into.

"Much as I appreciate the backup, Jak, we're not exactly winning the fight out here," she told him.

"Which is why we're here," he shot back, winking at her.

"The point was to keep you and your people out of it, remember?"

"Where's the honor it that, girl?" he asked. "I wouldn't be able to live with myself if all of you died and we lived on, skulking and hiding in the caves and getting by on dirt and refuse."

Taj couldn't blame him.

"Regardless, you're stepping out of the fire into a bigger fire," she went on, although she was sure she wasn't going to convince him to back out now.

He just shrugged, as she had thought he would. "What good is living on your knees if you're not willing to die on your feet?"

"You're just full of witticisms, aren't you?" Taj asked, chuckling.

"I've had a lot of time to think of stupid shit out here in the middle of nowhere," he answered with a chortling laugh. "A person gets to examining the details of everything if you're out here long enough. You start to think there's wisdom in it."

"Born and raised here, remember?" she shot back. "Trust me, I understand."

He grinned.

"Besides," he continued, "I was kinda hoping you had some kind of brilliant battle-ending plan you were holding onto for the last minute so you could come out on top looking glorious."

"Well, part of that is the case, although the brilliant part is debatable," she told him. "As for the waiting bit, that's only because gack isn't ready yet, not because I want to be dramatic."

Wyyvan fighters screamed overhead and Taj ducked out of reflex, but the shuttles kept them busy, forcing them to veer off without firing on the crew or the rebels.

She glanced toward the outpost and was grateful that Galforin had decided to try a more traditional approach to wiping them out than she'd expected.

Given her experiences with Captain Vort, Taj had imagined Galforin would run the artillery at full effect, cutting down enemy *and* friend in an effort to clear the field and end the battle that much sooner.

But she was starting to think that the admiral felt he needed his grunts and the workers as badly as Taj wanted to rescue the workers and rebels.

She'd decided it was because he needed the manpower.

He could throw his soldiers at them because he had ships loaded with more gliding through space at the moment, but it was clear that Galforin was being careful with his pieces, not just throwing them away with the board.

That played to her advantage, but it certainly wasn't winning them the war.

More of the Wyyvan fighters roared above, and Taj spared them a quick glance before looking at Dent.

"How much longer?" she asked.

He grinned. "Right about now," he told her, pointing at the fight happening just above them.

Taj stiffened and called to the combined forces of rebels and crew, "Now would be a damn good time to run for cover. Back to the tunnels! *Now*, gack it!"

The words barely out, a shuttle barreled into the midst of a mass of Wyyvan fighters, exploding as it drew close, a great ball of fire enveloping it and the pack of enemy ships.

A second one barreled into the midst of the Wyyvan advance.

A wash of brilliance blotted out the sky.

XO Volg bolted upright at his station, cursing.

Galforin spun. "XO?"

"Sorry, sir," he replied, salvaging his self-control, but

there was no mistaking the paleness of his green cheeks as examined his console.

"What is it?" the admiral questioned.

"There were massive explosions on the planet," Volg explained. "Both far beyond the capabilities of any of the forces positioned down there, friend or foe alike. They've temporarily blacked out our signals from the planet."

Galforin's heart sputtered and he tasted bile in the back of his throat. "Was it..."

Flashes of the worst-case scenario impaled his mind, and he felt a cold chill scamper down his spine.

"No, not that," Volg told him, but that only made the admiral feel *slightly* better.

"Then what?" Galforin pushed.

"It appears the invaders set off loads of the Toradium-42, sir," Volg answered, clearly disbelieving. "We lost five fighters in the blast, and untold foot soldiers."

Galforin swallowed hard, fighting back the taste of disgust that had crept to his tongue.

"How is that possible?"

"I don't know, Admiral," Volg said, the barest of trembles in his voice. "The spotty transmission link is making it hard for me to get a clear image of what happened. All I know is that they set off an explosion with the ore somehow, and its impact was devastating."

The admiral hissed, staring at his view screen, wishing he could compete with the technology of the cursed scum who'd invaded his planet. He had the numbers, but it was clear from the start that the enemy's confidence was unending.

They just kept coming, and Galforin had no idea why

or what they wanted other than to steal the Toradium-42 out from under him.

But even that didn't make sense when laid alongside the fact that the enemy could hardly be called an invasion force. They'd brought a pittance of soldiers and armament, and even the advantage of their AI couldn't overcome that kind of deficit.

Who are you, and what do you want?

"Scanners show eight shuttles returning to their command ship," Volg reported.

"Any lifeforms?" Galforin asked.

Volg grunted. "They're shielded, deflecting our scans. The ships are voids to our sensors."

"Could they be retreating from the planet?" the admiral wondered aloud.

That would be too much to hope for.

These creatures infuriated him. He had no clear understanding of what they wanted or why they were doing what they were doing, and it was causing him to second-guess himself and his decisions.

He'd already deferred to the XO once, and he felt he might do so again, showing Volg a weakness he didn't particularly want to reveal so plainly.

"Wait!" Volg cried out. "Not all of the shuttles returned to the command craft. They were using it for cover against our sensors. Four of them are following in the wake of a destroyer that's coming straight toward the fleet, sir."

Grand Admiral Galforin zoomed in on his screen, adjusting the angle to see the ship Volg was talking about. He saw one of the enemy destroyers hurtling straight toward the fleet. The four shuttles Volg mentioned advanced alongside it, flying in the shadows and using the larger ship's armor and shields to protect themselves from enemy fire.

"What are they doing?" he asked, although he wasn't sure if he was speaking to himself or his XO.

Volg swallowed so loudly that Galforin turned to look at the officer. "Sensors are picking up a concentration of Toradium-42 headed our direction. It's too large for their blocks to suppress."

"Where's it coming from?" Galforin asked, then the answer became obvious. "The shuttles."

Volg confirmed that a second later. "All four are carrying sufficient loads of the ore to—"

"Create the same kind of blackout that happened on the planet!" Galforin finished. "They're using the shuttles as bombs."

Volg barked a number of orders into the comm, but Galforin barely heard him.

"Retreat, Volg! Retreat," Galforin screamed, his throat raw at the intensity.

The *Stormfront* pulled away in haste, splitting off from the fleet without warning. The ship maneuvered at an angle that kept as many of the fleet's destroyers as possible between it and the incoming vessels.

The enemy destroyer struck first, driving its nose into the armored hull of a Wyyvan ship. The two crashed together, both firing as they tore apart at the impact. Debris and vented atmosphere obscured Galforin's view of the wreckage, although he could imagine it.

That would have to do since the shuttles veered off at the last second and flew straight at the nearest ships under the admiral's command. They reacted impressively, veering aside to avoid the shuttles, but maneuverability favored the smaller craft.

Worse still, they didn't even need to collide with the ships to bring their deadly load to bear.

All four of the shuttles exploded in unison and the *Stormfront*'s automatic dampeners blanked the screen, unable to deal with the intensity of the resulting blasts.

A shock wave washed over the *Stormfront* instants later, battering the dreadnought as Galforin struggled to remain seated within the tempest.

The ship listed and was carried off, its engines failing.

CHAPTER TWELVE

Taj and the others wasted no time darting for the cover of the many gullies the Wyyvan mining venture had ripped in the surface of Krawlas.

Dent had assured her that the explosions were positioned well enough, their energies contained so as to not harm the rebels or the crew, but Taj wasn't taking any chances.

She understood how powerful the mineral was, and when she had suggested using it as a weapon, she'd had a good idea of what she was asking for.

The reality, however, far exceeded the theory.

The sky had turned white for an instant, blacking out all communication and nearly blinding the crew. If they hadn't been turned away from the blast, there might well have been permanent damage done to their eyes. As it was, the concussive shock sent those at the rear of their ranks tumbling.

There'd be a lot of bruised and sore people in the morning.

If they survive the night, Taj corrected.

Once they'd recovered from the blast, they slipped away, returning to the rebel tunnels. Taj sighed, grateful to crawl into the dark, deep cavern, as far from the Wyyvan soldiers as possible.

Given what they'd been through, a comforting sense of peace settled over her, and Taj reveled in it for the few seconds it lasted.

Malcolm ran up to them, wide-eyed and sweaty, grit and dirt clinging to his cheeks and filling the wrinkles in his forehead.

"What happened?"

"Later," Jak said to Malcolm, still blinking away the aftereffects of the blast.

Taj could only imagine how uncomfortable it must have been to not have solid eye protection while out there. He had to be seeing all sorts of dancing dots.

Malcolm seemed to take the dismissal in stride, choosing to say nothing.

"Is the work done?" Jak asked.

"It is," he answered, wiping the dirt from his brow. "The tunnels extend all the way under the compound, coming up in all the locations you ordered. All that's needed is to punch through the last few layers of ground, and we're inside."

Taj grunted her approval.

"Our people in place?" Jak asked with a grim smile.

"They are."

"Then let's get going," he said. "Once those soldiers recover, they're going to be out for blood."

Taj didn't argue.

They'd effectively set off a tactical nuke in the middle of Wyyvan fighters. She could only imagine the carnage they'd left behind on the field.

Actually, she didn't want to imagine it.

Some things are better left as mysteries, she thought.

The crew and rebels raced into the tunnels that Jak's people had dug while the rest battled in the desert above. Cabe caught up to Taj.

"That was one gack of a distraction," he told her. "Remind me not to make you mad."

"You need to worry about Dent, not me," she said, laughing. "It was my idea, but he's the one who made everything go boom."

"It's a surprisingly simply process, I have to admit," the AI told them. "I'm truly amazed that the Wyyvans hadn't yet figured it out and used their foothold here against us."

"Let's keep that secret to ourselves," Krawg said, shaking his shaggy head. "I feel like I've got a sunburn despite my fur and the armor."

"The blast had one gack of a kick," Torbon admitted.

"Imagine what can be done with processed and refined Toradium-42," Lina said, whistling.

"Not sure I want to," Torbon answered. "To be honest, I'd be perfectly happy going back to a time when I'd never heard of the stuff. Life was pretty good before we were living on an energy source that could blow the planet up with enough of it."

"That's a scary thought," Taj whispered, trying not to think about it.

The rebels and crew split between the tunnels. Taj, Cabe, Torbon, Lina, Dent, and Krawg, along with Jak and Rat, came to the end of their tunnel a short while later. A handful of rebels were there, hovering around one of the tunneling machines and pacing impatiently. Jak greeted them.

He turned back and looked at Taj once he was done. "Any reason for us to wait?"

"Best we don't," she advised. "The quicker we take advantage of the chaos above, the better our chances of pulling this off are."

"Fair enough," Jak replied, motioning to his people.

They pulled on masks to protect them from the dust and triggered the machine, moving it into position and digging away the last few feet of solid ground between them and the outpost above.

Artificial light shined down on them as the ground gave way, and Taj and the others bolted from the angled tunnel into the night.

They emerged just west of an artillery unit with two soldiers on duty there.

The lizards gaped at seeing them appear out of the ground and died immediately afterward.

Both collapsed in a heap, and two of the rebels set upon the cannon, familiarizing themselves with it as a small contingent of Jak's people scattered down nearby alleys and streets to find and free workers. A group stuck with Taj.

"Next," Torbon said, gesturing in a different direction. He started off without waiting for them.

Taj and the others followed him.

The rebels' main mission was to gather the workers and lead them to the various tunnels, getting them ready to flee the compound while Taj and her outfit captured and converted as many of the artillery units to their own use as they could before the Wyyvan soldiers outside figured things out.

As had been the case from the start, the clock was against them.

Taj and the others raced through the outpost, following the pseudo-map she'd drawn up after riding along on the automated vehicle and the intel of the rebels. While she was sure they'd missed some of the artillery units, they had a good idea where most of them were.

Better still, the Wyyvans' confidence in their reconnection with Galforin and the push outside of the walls had unintentionally benefited Taj's mission.

With fewer soldiers at each weapon, the majority out on the plains hunting the cats and rebels, the units were easier to take over. The number of soldiers guarding the workers had been reduced too, and they'd been corralled in fewer areas to maximize the effectiveness of the guards who remained.

That made the Wyyvans easier targets.

Taj came across another artillery station and ran straight at it. Communications down, they had no clue that a half-dozen of the weapons had already been commandeered. The lizards hung around their post almost causally, awaiting an order to start firing that would never come.

Taj shot the first lizard in the back of the head, driving him face-first into the artillery mount. Stunned, he growled and tried to regain his senses.

The other Wyyvan soldier spun around, raising his weapon only to meet the full force of the others. He was gunned down by the crew, stumbling back and only falling once they'd stopped pulling their triggers.

As the other scrambled to his feet, Taj came up behind him and blew a hole in his back from point-blank range. He died without a sound, having never fully regained his wits.

Taj hopped on the comm once they took another of the artillery positions.

"All gun units, turn your fire on the killing field just outside the outpost's walls and slowly expand from there," she ordered.

Torbon looked at the night sky, eyes narrow. "Now's the moment of truth, huh?"

Taj nodded as the various artillery units under their control began to fire, filling the darkness with blazing fury.

"The Wyyvan fleet has pulled back, although they've yet to break off hostilities," Dent reported. "Our stunt with the Toradium-42 caught them off-guard, just as it did down here. They lost four ships to the explosion, and the blast has scrambled communications."

"That still leaves us at a deficit up there." Taj sighed. "Can the Wyyvans still hit us from where they are?"

"Unfortunately, they can," Dent admitted. "They are still within firing range of the planet."

"So once they figure out that we're using their artillery against their own people…" Torbon let his sentence fade.

Everyone knew the consequences of dropping straight into the middle of the contained target that was the outpost. It was why the rebels needed to move fast to get the workers into the tunnels and away from the outpost before Galforin's restraint surrendered to his fury.

It was a balancing act.

"Jak!" Taj called over the comm. "How's it going?"

The rebel leader's voice came back quickly. "We've recovered most of the workers and are moving them to the tunnel entrances. Waiting for more cover fire from the artillery units before we start moving."

Taj nodded although she knew Jak couldn't see her. "Keep doing what you're doing, but if you could do it quicker, that'd be a good idea."

"Roger that!" Jak replied and cut the call.

Taj expected a rain of ship's fire on her head any moment, and the longer it took to arrive, the more worried she became.

They took down another three artillery units while they waited.

The Wyyvan soldiers at the first unit put up a perfunctory fight, but those at the others had apparently figured out where their fellow units had started dropping their munitions and realized they were on the losing side of a battle they hadn't even known was going on.

When the crew approached the units, the Wyyvan soldiers were retreating or had already fled, trying to escape the enemy they knew were inside the walls now.

"This is too easy," Cabe complained. "I thought they'd put up a more determined fight to keep their positions."

"We got lucky," Taj said, and she felt that was truly the case.

She hadn't been as prepared to fight a war as she'd thought; working off old intel, not knowing the lay of the land; she'd come in blind, and she'd had to think on the fly.

Fortunately, the pieces had fallen into place after the Toradium-42 explosions. She'd sent the Wyyvans reeling, and they'd yet to recover.

They would eventually, though.

She and the crew had to be gone by then.

"Get those guns firing so we can clear a perimeter around the outpost, then we're out of here," she ordered.

"The troops on the field are moving back and taking cover where they can," Dent reported, using the remaining shuttles to keep an eye on the battle.

The Wyyvan fighter squadron had mostly been destroyed in the blast and the resulting confusion, Dent's automated shuttles unaffected by the explosion they had known was coming.

They'd cleaned up the majority of the fighters and were hunting down the last of the them while the Wyyvan artillery swept through the rank-and-file soldiers on the ground.

Taj glanced at the sky, something she and the others had done regularly since they'd started trying to take the outpost.

"Not that I mind, but why the gack hasn't Galforin started pelting us?" she asked.

Dent didn't have an answer.

"Is this place that important?" Lina wondered.

"How important could it be if he's lost it?" Cabe countered.

"Fleet status," Taj asked the AI.

"Still fighting us and holding strong," he reported. "The Wyyvans on the field are moving out of artillery range and reforming their lines."

"We're all in position," Jak told her over the comm. "Moving the workers through the tunnels now."

"Be careful," she answered. "See you soon."

Outside of the blast of the artillery units and the occasional flurry of small-arms fire as the rebels came across pockets of Wyyvan resistance, the outpost was eerily quiet.

The lizards had largely given up the fight.

That didn't sit well with Taj.

"Something is wrong," she muttered.

"Why?" Torbon asked. "Because things are going so well."

Taj chuckled. "That's part of it, yeah."

Although she felt that it was stupid to fret about success, she couldn't help but think that their victory had been too easy.

Her stomach churned with apprehension.

"Could we have walked into a trap?" she asked.

"If so, why haven't they sprung it yet?" Dent replied.

Taj shrugged. That was part of the problem. Nothing made sense to her. She simply couldn't picture them having won so easily.

"They couldn't have known what we planned," Lina added. "Maybe we just keep surprising them? Keeping them on their heels, off-guard?"

"Maybe," Taj agreed, but she couldn't shake the feeling that the hammer was waiting to fall on their heads.

"We've got movement across the killing field," Dent called. "Four Wyyvan soldiers waving a flag of truce." One of his eyebrows rose in surprise. "They're carrying a device with them."

"A weapon?" Cabe asked.

The AI shook his head. "Looks like a loudspeaker," he replied. "An archaic communications device, nothing more."

"Cease fire," Taj ordered the artillery units to keep them from blowing the approaching soldiers away. "Let them approach."

"You sure about that?" Torbon asked.

She sighed at the question. "What are four soldiers going to do that the fleet hovering over our head can't?" she asked him.

Taj knew she should be worried about the Wyyvans' sudden capitulation, but she was more curious than anything. She wanted to know what they were up to, and the way to find out was to let things play out for now.

A few moments later, the Wyyvan soldiers had set up their device and began broadcasting.

"This is Grand Admiral Galforin of the Wyyvan fleet, overseer of planet KI1047-32," a voice called over the loud-speaker. Taj grated at hearing him so callously claim control of her home world, but she bit back her anger to hear him out. "I wish to speak with the commander of the invaders who dared usurp my mining operation."

The admiral went on, offering them a private communication channel Taj could use to reach him on his dread-nought before cutting the connection.

Taj looked at Dent, who shrugged.

"Maybe he wants to surrender?" Torbon suggested.

Taj looked at the sky one last time and snarled. "He's buying time," she said, more to herself than anyone else. "Let's see what he has to say, Dent. Open a channel."

Galforin was playing at something, and she wanted to know what.

CHAPTER THIRTEEN

Dent patched the private communication through the small device built into his wrist. It had a narrow screen, and the AI held it up to face Taj.

After being assured that Galforin couldn't trace the transmission back to the source, using it to target them, she stood in front of a blank wall with no identifying marks to make it even harder for the admiral to determine where in the outpost they were.

Galforin's green countenance appeared on the screen, looking sour. He licked his lips in distaste as he saw who was on the other side of the connection.

Taj had removed her helmet to look the lizard in the eyes. She'd waited a long time for this moment.

"Ah," Galforin said, nodding. "It all makes sense now. You're Furlorian."

"We gacking well are!" she told him. "Did you think we were gonna just let you have our planet?" she fired back, letting her anger get the best of her.

"I did, actually," he told her, smirking. "Especially after you ran away so quickly, abandoning it with your tails between your legs."

Taj wanted to reach through the screen and scratch his eyes out.

"We've got your outpost under our control," she said, trying not to let the lizard's smugness get to her. "Your whole purpose for being here is shut down, so why don't you just call it a loss and move on? You won't get a second chance to take it."

He shook his head. "I don't think so, rodent. In fact, I've reached out to you to demand your surrender," he stated. "Give up now, and I'll spare the lives of you and your people and the slaves on the planet. Choose to continue in this foolish effort to take KI1047-32 from me, and I'll punish you on every front."

"You mean like how you did when we sent your fleet and soldiers running with *their* tails between *their* legs?" she shot back.

Galforin snarled at her before reining his anger in. She was getting under his skin, and she liked it.

"Believe what you will, Furlorian, but you and I both know you don't have the upper hand. You barely have enough forces to put up a token show of effort, let alone win back your planet," he told her. "It's only a matter of time before we overwhelm you and add you to the slaves mining Toradium-42 for us. Give in to the inevitable and surrender. It will save your people torment."

Taj laughed at his offer. "Why not just blow the compound and take us out?" she pressed. "The fact that you haven't tells me you're not as confident about the outcome as you'd like me to believe."

"I'm nothing if not generous, rodent," he returned, grinning, but Taj could see the forced nature of it.

He was hiding something.

Taj wanted to know what.

"Yeah, I'm sure that's what it's all about, Galforin," she told him. "I mean, you were clearly very generous to Vort, raining down all that extra firepower to help him out when you first arrived."

"I'm not the one who tossed him into space to die," the admiral countered.

Taj grinned. "I shot him in the head first if that makes you feel better," she explained. "Maybe you and I should sit down and talk in person and see which of us can *negotiate* the better deal."

"Tempting," Galforin told her, "but you only have the two options I've offered you: Surrender and live or fight and die. Your choice, but make up your mind quickly." He leaned into the screen, his already sizable face growing even larger, looming across the distance. "I'll be in touch soon, Furlorian. Choose wisely."

The Wyyvan admiral cut the connection and Dent pulled his arm back.

"That told us nothing," Torbon complained.

"Actually, it told us quite a bit," Dent replied.

"He doesn't think he can kill us," Taj stated, glancing at the sky again, imagining she could see the admiral stewing in his ship. "He's worried about something, or he'd simply blow us up and get back to work, especially now that he knows how few of us there really are."

"What could he be worried about?" Cabe asked.

"That's what we need to find out," Taj told him.

Static filled the comm then and Jak's voice came through, chaos distorting the call.

"They've found our tunnels!" he screamed over the link. "The Wyyvans are blowing them up, collapsing them ahead of us. We're pulling back."

Taj snarled. "Gack!"

"Could this be what he was waiting for?" Lina asked.

"I don't know." Taj shrugged. "Maybe he was buying time to get his people in place."

"If that's the case, we only have a short while before everyone is back in the compound, allowing Galforin to take us all out at once."

"Have the armada keep an eye on his weapons systems, Dent," Taj told the AI. "If he turns anything our way, we need to know as soon as possible."

She paced in a tight circle, wondering if she'd made a mistake by corralling all of them in one place.

The walls of the compound had been compromised so it would be difficult to hold them against a concentrated effort by the Wyyvans, but they'd have to make it across the killing field first. With access to the artillery units now, that would make a push on the outpost difficult no matter how many Wyyvans Galforin had at his disposal.

Unfortunately, she'd shown the aliens that Toradium-42 could be weaponized and turned against her and the crew, but that would take time.

"What do you want to do?" Cabe asked. "If he was looking to get us all in here together, it won't be long before something bad happens."

Taj nodded, head whirling with thoughts. Although she had no idea what the gack Galforin had planned, she understood the first thing she needed to do was find a safe way out of the outpost.

"Come in, Rat!" she called.

The young woman's voice came back a moment later. "Here!"

"How far are you from the outpost?"

"Haven't left," she answered. "Was overseeing the retreat with Malcolm."

Taj grunted. That was a good thing, at least.

"Then I need you to do something," Taj told her. "Get some people and get back on those mining devices and dig us new tunnels out of here. To the west would probably be our best bet to avoid further interference by the lizards. Can you do that?"

There was a momentary pause, and Taj assumed the girl was conferring with Malcolm. Taj waited impatiently as the seconds ticked by, then Rat came back.

"We're on it, Taj," the girl answered.

"The sooner, the better," Taj suggested.

"You got it," Rat said, and the comm went silent.

"You think there's time for that?" Lina asked.

Taj shrugged. "The devices are quick. If we can get them up and running again right away, it gives us a chance."

"My main concern is what is keeping Galforin from destroying the outpost," Dent stated, glancing around.

"Could he simply not want to waste his time rebuilding?" Cabe asked.

"I don't know," Taj answered. "It could be. He's kept the

tech at low levels to avoid drawing attention to his efforts here, so maybe that's all it is. A round of heavy fire on the planet, and the resultant effort to rebuild might be more than he wants to advertise his operation."

"If that were the case, our battle above and the explosions would have far exceeded that threshold for emitting energy signals," Dent explained. "Which makes me think it's something else."

"Well, *we* didn't want to destroy the place from orbit because of the workers trapped here," Lina said, "so what's here that *he* doesn't want to risk blowing up?"

Taj turned to stare at the engineer, eyes narrow. "There's nothing here," she mused. "Dent has scanned the area, and he's found nothing but low-tech mechanical devices. There's nothing he can't replace, including the workers. I wouldn't put it past him to put his soldiers to work if he needed them to, like Vort did."

Lina shrugged. "Nothing else makes sense, though," she argued.

"Maybe he's just on so tight a schedule that he can't afford to start over," Cabe offered.

"We're wasting our time speculating," Taj told them. "Our priority is to get out of the complex and then get off-planet. Let's join Rat and Malcolm and see if we can help dig an exit we can use."

Taj didn't give them the opportunity to argue. She started off, stomping off toward where Rat would be setting up the devices.

Something was going on that she didn't understand, and she hated it.

It felt like the world was ready to come crashing down on their heads at any moment.

But Taj hadn't come all this way to lose her home again.

She'd figured out a way to get them off the Plains and into the complex against all odds. She sure as gack wouldn't fail at finding a way out.

It had been a couple of hours since Taj had spoken to Galforin, and she was hot and dirty and hated the taste of the grit that had settled between her teeth.

While Dent kept an eye on the fleet above, ready to warn of imminent destruction, she and the others had jumped in to help Rat and Malcolm drill new tunnels out of the compound.

Although she still wasn't sure what she was going to do once they emerged, seeing as how the rebel hideout had been compromised, she felt more comfortable being out in the open. At least there they could run and hide; split up and vanish from the enemy fleet in the desert or Everon's Canyon.

From there, they could take the remaining shuttles back to the fleet and wreak havoc on Galforin's operations on the planet.

It wasn't much of a plan, but it was all she had.

One problem at a time, she told herself.

She wondered if Mama Merr and Gran Beaux had ever felt this way.

Of course they had, she thought. There was no way they

could rule over all of the surviving Furlorians and not feel as if their mistakes would bring down ruin.

At least with the majority of her people still on Corzant and a secret backup of Dent's Dandrinite knowledge left behind just in case, Taj felt as if all wouldn't be lost should she fail to retake Krawlas.

"I guess this is good practice for when the lizards recapture us," Rat joked, nudging Taj from her sour reverie.

The young female had worked alongside Taj ever since they'd joined her and she hadn't complained once.

"An optimist, I see," Torbon muttered.

"We're all going to end up in the dirt one day anyway, so what difference does *when* make?" she asked.

"A whole lot," Taj countered. She still had a whole bunch of living left to do. "And none of us are gonna end up dying in here."

"How can you be so sure?" Rat asked.

"Because we're not done fighting," Taj told the girl. "As long as we keep standing up again every time we get knocked down, we'll win."

"Now who's the optimist?" Torbon teased.

"It's that or curl up and die," Taj shot back. "And I don't know about you, but I'm sure not ready to die at the hands of some lizard who thinks he has the right to invade our home and take it away from our people."

"Hear, hear!" Cabe called. "Gack that lizard."

"Besides, General Reynolds wants a new pair of boots," Lina added. "I bet he'd appreciate a nice new belt, too."

Rat chuckled and turned back to her work as the tunneling device began to rumble. She adjusted the controls, but the sound grew louder and louder.

"What is that?" Taj asked.

"It's acting like we're about to break through the surface, but that can't be right," Rat explained.

"Could there be something there we didn't know about?" Lina wondered.

Rat nodded and eased back on the throttle, slowing the device. "Who knows what the Wyyvans did before we arrived? There could be all sorts of tunnels under here." She fought with the device. "I'm redirecting us away from this softer patch to see if—"

She didn't get the last of her statement out before there was a loud crack and the wall gave way in front of the tunneling machine.

Dust rose up in a cloud, and the whole front of the machine was buried in an avalanche of dirt and debris as it punched a hole into an adjoining chamber.

Rat leaped back, waving at the dust so she could get a better look at what happened.

With her advanced optics, Taj had a clear view of what had transpired. Her heart sputtered in her chest at the sight.

She clambered over and peered through the hole. A massive cavern loomed before her, filled nearly to the ceiling with piles of Toradium-42. The mineral stretched into the distance as far as she could see.

"Oh...gack!" she mumbled, stepping back out of instinct. "I think I know why Galforin hasn't fired on us."

CHAPTER FOURTEEN

Grand Admiral Galforin paced his bridge. It had become a ritual he hated.

"Those worthless rodents," he growled.

He'd underestimated their tenacity, much as he imagined Captain Vort had. That had landed the captain dead in space, and Galforin had no desire to join him.

But there was little he could do at the moment, and that fed his fury.

"The soldiers are in place," XO Volg informed him. "They'll siphon as much of the Toradium-42 from the storage chambers as possible while the Furlorians wait for you to contact them again."

Galforin chuckled. "Do you really think they're passively waiting around for me to reach out, XO?" he asked. "Would *you*?"

Volg shook his head. "No, sir."

"Exactly," Galforin barked. "They know we're holding

back for a reason, even if they don't know what that reason is. It will only be a matter of time before they find another way out or they stumble across our cache of Toradium-42."

"Why not just let them go, sir?" Volg asked. "Wouldn't it be best to have them away from the ore and off-planet?"

"If I believed they would stay away, I'd agree with you, Volg. But these rodents have shown themselves to be quite persistent," he said. "I can't foresee any circumstance where we are able to strip the planet and get away with our prize before either the Furlorians return again to re-engage us or Command learns what we are doing out here. With such limited resources, we can't afford any more delays, Volg."

"But if we return to Belor Prime with the ore we already have mined, won't that be enough for you to buy your seat on the Council?" the XO wondered.

Galforin nodded. "It would be—until the Council determined that haul was the barest drop in a bucket of the resources this planet has to offer. They would steal it from us without hesitation." Galforin grunted. "Then what do you think would happen to us, Volg?"

The XO sneered. "No need to ask, Admiral," he replied. "Command would have us executed."

"Exactly," Galforin shot back and made his way to his seat. He dropped down with a huff. "How long before the ore is removed from the chamber and we can safely fire upon the outpost?"

"Days," Volg answered. "A week possibly, as long as we are not delayed by the Furlorians."

Galforin growled low in his throat. He'd made a mistake storing all the Toradium-42 in a single location, but he had wanted it where he could best control it. There hadn't been so much as an inkling in his mind that the Furlorians would return to reclaim their planet, let alone that they would manage to take the outpost from under him. He'd been so careful not to draw any outside interest into his operation on the planet.

But now that the Furlorians had come back, there was nothing he could do as long as the ore remained concentrated under the outpost.

As the Furlorians had deduced, Toradium-42 was volatile under certain circumstances. In such a concentration, were Galforin to ignite it with weapons fire from the *Stormfront*, he would set off a chain reaction that would engulf the entire planet, destroying any chance he had of harvesting more ore.

There would simply be nothing left of KI1047-32.

"Our forces are making their way under the outpost as we speak, sir," Volg went on, clearly trying to remain positive. "If nothing else, we can throw our troops at them on the surface; push through the broken walls and run them down."

"That might be our only choice, XO," Galforin admitted, although he hated to.

Throwing his forces at the Furlorians, especially now that they controlled the artillery, would result in him losing far too many of his people. And with no certainty that he could slip past the Furlorian armada and get his reinforcements on the ground safely, he would have no one to work the mines until he was able to collect more slaves.

That would take time he didn't believe he had available.

But his options dwindled the longer he waited to make a decision.

He needed to do something.

Soon.

CHAPTER FIFTEEN

"Bloody Rowl!" Cabe cursed, staring at the mass of Toradium-42 stockpiled beneath the compound.

"It seems to me that the Wyyvan admiral knew full well the explosive capability of Toradium-42," Dent said, motioning to the chamber.

"He's afraid to blow it all up," Taj added, realizing that was why Galforin had been so quick to offer terms and hadn't come after them with everything he had when the opportunity was there. "How much damage do you think lighting all this up at once would do?"

"The resultant explosion would obliterate the planet," Dent replied, assessing the amount of Toradium-42 in the chamber. "A detonation of that magnitude would likely ignite all of the mineral veins running through Krawlas, creating a massive chain reaction. There would be nothing left of the planet but debris."

"Well, at least we now know he isn't going to nuke us from orbit," Torbon offered.

"Hardly a comfort," Lina muttered. "He'll figure out some other way to come at us because there's no way in gack he's gonna leave this much Toradium-42 behind."

"But it gives us time to figure another way out, at least," Taj said, looking at the brighter side of their revelation.

"Not sure that's the case," Jak said, coming over to join them. "My people on the walls report that the Wyyvan forces are advancing slowly, moving into position to attack."

"He's going to throw his people at us, looking to over-whelm our defenses and get inside the outpost," Cabe reasoned. "If that happens, there's no way we can hold them off."

"What about the artillery?" Krawg questioned.

"It'll earn its keep," Taj said, "but there's no way it will keep them from breaching the walls."

"So, we made it this far just to die, huh?" Malcolm asked, growling. "There's no way we can get new tunnels dug before the Wyyvans breach the walls."

"What about your remaining shuttles?" Jak asked. "Can they ferry us back to your fleet?"

"It'd take a number of trips, but it's viable," Dent replied.

"They're being used for something else," Taj countered, shaking her head.

"What do you mean?" Malcolm snapped. "You *trying* to get us killed, cat? What could possibly be more important than flying us outta here?"

"I've told you before, this is our planet," she explained again. "We won't abandon it unless it's absolutely necessary."

"Seems to me being surrounded and outnumbered and

outgunned is a damn good reason to take the last chance we have of escaping seriously, don't you think?" Malcolm told her.

"There's no certainty we'd make it back to the armada, let alone get out of the system and away from the Wyyvan fleet if we run now," she argued.

"Sounds like a way better chance than waiting until the damn lizards raid the outpost," he shot back.

"I have to agree," Jak stated. "You're holding onto hope, and I get it, but it doesn't seem rational. We need to get out of here or we're all going to die."

"You don't get to make these decisions for us," Malcolm added.

Taj sighed, torn between her need to free the planet from Wyyvan control and rescue the rebels.

Were they to run now, they would lose their chance at redemption, but she had a chance to save Jak and Rat and the rest of the people who'd been trapped on the planet under the Wyyvans' whip.

That's something I can consider a victory, right?

It was, but there was no way she would ever be able to reconcile her feelings if she were to flee and leave the planet behind.

It had been her choice to abandon it the first time, but she'd be gacked if she did it again.

Taj shook her head.

"I can offer your people a way off the planet and out of the system, but not until I've made arrangements to retake our planet," she stated, not leaving any room for argument. "I need all my shuttles and ships until then."

"So we're just supposed to wait around and try not to die until you're done playing the hero?" Malcolm shouted.

He inched forward and was met by Cabe stepping up to keep him from getting any closer to Taj. She set a restraining hand on Cabe's tense shoulder, keeping him from hurting the older rebel.

Malcolm got the hint and backed off, but his fury didn't lessen.

"You're going to get us all killed, cat," he spat. "Your impossible quest to defeat the lizards is going to be a bloody footnote to the history of this planet, and ain't nobody going to remember what you did here because there won't be nobody alive to care.

"You're making a mistake, and I won't let my people suffer for it." He spun on his heel and stomped down the tunnel.

Jak swallowed hard, looking like he planned to say something, then decided not to. He looked away and followed Malcolm. All of their people except Rat left too. The young female watched them leave, only turning to look back at Taj once they were gone.

"You sure about this?" she asked.

"She *really* hates that question," Torbon advised the girl.

"I'm not sure of anything, Rat," Taj answered. "All I know is that I didn't come all this way to lose my home a second time. If there's a chance we can take it back, I need to try."

Rat stared at her for a moment before conceding with a nod. "I understand, and I'll try to talk to Jak and Malcolm," she said. "Don't think it will do much good, but I believe we're better off working out a solution together than we are apart."

"I completely agree," Taj told her.

Rat gave a quick wave and ran after her people. An uncomfortable silence settled over the crew for a few minutes before the engineer broke it.

"What do you think Malcolm meant by his comment?" Lina asked. "Was it a threat?"

"They'd be stupid to fight us," Torbon stated. "We would wipe them out."

"But we don't want to, is the point," Taj told him. "That's not who we are. If we have to choose between rescuing them or killing them to keep Krawlas, that's no decision at all. We can't hurt these people to get our home back."

"But they don't have the right to stop us from trying," Torbon argued.

"We involved them by coming here," Taj said. "We didn't give them a choice in the matter, dragging them into the fight and putting their lives at risk. We don't have the right to expect anything of them, Torbon, especially not that they lay down their lives for a planet that's not even their own."

"The Wyyvans brought them here, not us," he shot back. "This isn't our fault. We need to do what we came here for."

"You're right, and we will, but not at the cost of their lives," Taj told him flat out. She turned to Dent. "How many operational shuttles do we have left?"

"We have ten, plus the four that remain upon the *Decimator*," he answered.

Taj nodded. "Recall those four with the supplies we

need and get them down here as soon as possible," she ordered.

"And the rest?" Dent asked.

"I have a plan," she told him.

"That's never a good thing," Krawg muttered.

"The last couple have worked out okay, haven't they?" Taj asked.

"Well, if you count almost searing everyone's eyes out, sure," Krawg replied, giving her a toothy grin. "I won't mention them trapping us in here with a mountain of Toradium-42."

Lina groaned. "Except that you just did."

"Okay, so maybe the plans haven't been spectacular up to this point," Taj admitted, "but we're still alive, right?"

"For now," Torbon answered.

"Alive is alive," she argued. "The goal is to make sure we stay that way."

She turned back to the AI and Lina. "Here's what I want you to do…"

Taj explained her idea to the pair, and the rest of the crew listened, eyes wide, taking it all in.

She didn't know if her plan would work, especially after what she'd done the last time around, but they were running out of options. She needed to do something bold and brash or they would find themselves overrun by the Wyyvans with nothing to show for their efforts but death.

Taj wasn't ready to quit. She was willing to die to reclaim Krawlas for her people, but she wouldn't unduly risk the lives of the rebels to accomplish it.

"Find Jak and let him know what we've decided," she told Cabe.

He nodded and started off.

Her idea was a compromise, giving the rebels a chance at freedom and a new life while offering Taj an opportunity to use them to the crew's benefit.

She felt a little guilty about her decision, but she couldn't see another way out of this without taking a chance. She'd do everything in her power to ensure the escaping rebels weren't hurt by her choices.

At the end of the day, that was all she could do.

A tense hush had settled over the crew after Cabe had informed Jak and his people what they were going to do.

Jak had joined the crew, and they gathered in one of the tunnels as the drilling machine worked its way toward freedom outside the outpost. Taj had had Dent plot a course for the shuttles so they would meet up with the rebels once they broke through but not before.

They didn't want to reveal the location of their tunnels until the very last moment.

Besides, she had other plans for them.

She glanced at Dent with questioning eyes and the AI nodded, letting her know everything was going as they'd arranged.

Taj looked at Jak then. He'd come around and joined them in the tunnel once his part of the plan had been explained. Malcolm hadn't been as agreeable, but Taj hadn't expected him to be.

"You're truly going to give us one of your destroyers?" the rebel leader asked.

Taj nodded. "We understand that we put you in this situation, and you deserve a way out that doesn't involve you dying for a planet that's not your home."

"And all we need to do is ride up in the shuttles to the other craft before joining the rest in the destroyer you're giving us?"

"Yup," she replied. "There's a chance, however, that the Wyyvan admiral might not want you to leave and take steps to stop you."

"We'll take that risk," he told her, drawing in a deep breath before letting it out slowly. "For what it's worth, I admire your conviction."

She laughed. "Even if it gets everyone killed?"

"I didn't say I thought your idea was a good one, but I admire your willingness to do everything you can to take your home back from these lizard bastards." He paused a moment before continuing, "I'm sorry we can't do more to help you."

"No need to apologize," she replied. "You've done enough. This isn't your fight. You shouldn't have to stick around and get yourselves killed for this place. Your people deserve their freedom."

"We're almost there," Rat called from her post at the tunneling machine. "Won't be long now."

Jak acknowledged her with a smile and looked at Taj again. "I'll go let my people know."

He started down the tunnel, and Taj turned back to watch Rat plowing her way through the planet. It amazed her how easy the devices made it look, displacing millions of metric tons of dirt and rock and disintegrating it to keep the way behind the machine clear.

If they managed to free Krawlas, Taj could see a host of uses for these devices.

Her gaze trailed the wall as she contemplated, and a flutter of movement in the shadows of the tunnel caught her eye. She glanced back and saw one of the rebels race up to Jak before he'd cleared the tunnel. The male was clearly out of breath.

He got close to Jak and said something into the man's ear. The rebel leader stiffened, and the two raced off without another word.

"That was…odd," Dent mused, apparently have seen the same thing Taj had.

Taj agreed. She tapped Lina on the shoulder to get her attention. "You guys stay here and monitor the tunneling," she told the engineer. "We're gonna get check on something real quick."

Lina, having not seen the strange exchange between Jak and his partner, shrugged and did as she was asked.

But after Malcolm's threat, Taj wasn't sure she was entirely ready to trust all the rebels. Something was clearly going on, and she decided she needed to know what it was in case it impacted her plan.

There was barely any chance of success as it was, and she sure as gack wasn't going to allow some petty scheme by Malcolm or the other rebels to compromise it.

She triggered her camo program, Dent doing the same, and the two crept down the tunnel after Jak.

Fortunately, with everyone working in the various tunnels, they didn't have many people to avoid until they caught up with Jak.

The two stopped in the middle of a tunnel that had

been excavated well before the current location, but it only took a second for her to realize something was wrong.

The rebel pointed, and Jak put his hand against the wall. His eyes widened, and Taj caught a glimpse of dust swirling above his head.

Jak cursed and shot toward the far end of the tunnel, his guy following him. Taj and Dent waited until they were gone before going over to where they stood, examining the wall as Jak had.

They knew immediately what was going on.

"Gack!" Taj muttered under her breath.

"It seems the Wyyvans are making their way toward us," Dent said, tapping the wall with a finger. "They appear to be digging parallel to this tunnel, but reverberations in the wall tell me there are other tunnels being dug that are not the ones our people are creating."

"How can you tell?" Taj asked, not that she doubted the AI. She just didn't understand how he could know all that.

"My systems can mimic the effect of the seismic devices, although at a much-reduced range," he explained. "I'm monitoring the direction of the tunnels that are being dug nearby, and this one on the other side of the wall, and one other that I can detect are moving in the opposite direction of the tunnels our people are drilling."

"And since we aren't drilling in circles, it's not us." Taj caught on, sighing. "How long do we have?"

"Not long," Dent told her. "Given the trajectory of the tunnels they're digging, if they remain constant, the Wyyvans will spill into the middle of our network of tunnels, trapping many of our people on the wrong end of them."

"Gacking Rowl!" she spat. "We need to warn everyone."

"There might not be time to get them out of the tunnels," he advised. "Besides, if they *do* make it, that would place us back in the outpost, caught between the Wyyvans tunneling to us and those ready to press from the outside."

Taj pictured the scenario and realized there would be no way out for any of them if that happened. The lizards would crush them and there would be nothing they could do about it.

"Gack it!" she exclaimed. "Open that channel to Galforin. Hail him."

Dent did as he was asked, raising his screen so the admiral could see Taj when and if, he decided to accept the hail.

Several moments crept by with no response before Galforin's wide face appeared on the screen.

"Chosen to surrender, have you?" he asked, a smirk peeling his green lips back. "Excellent decision."

Taj got straight to the point.

"Pull your forces back and stop tunneling under the outpost or I'll blow your cache of Toradium-42, Galforin."

The admiral barely managed to keep from gasping. "What—"

"Don't play stupid, Galforin," she pressed. "We know about your stockpile of the mineral under the outpost. If you don't pull your people back and stop trying to come after us, we will blow it up, and all your reason for being here with it."

"You wouldn't dare," he exclaimed. "You would destroy your planet, and you right along with it."

"You're gonna kill us anyway, right?" she fired back. "At

least this way I know you get nothing out of the deal, not even the satisfaction of knowing we're dead, seeing as how we'd be taking everything with us."

Galforin stiffened, his upper lip quivering. "I took you for foolish, Furlorian, but not suicidal."

"Desperate times call for desperate measures, Admiral," she said. "You're pushing us into a corner, so don't be surprised when we lash out because we don't have any other options."

Galforin stared at her as if trying to see inside her mind. She met his eyes with a steely gaze, willing him to believe her every word.

It was a bluff. Taj no more willing to blow up the planet than Galforin was, but she had to convince him. She had to make him think she would do exactly that.

"Do you think your fleet's far enough away to avoid the planetary explosion, Admiral?" she pushed. "I don't think it is, even with that Gate up there. You'd have to get back to it first. Not much time."

Galforin said nothing.

Taj motioned off-camera, although there was no one there. "Light it up," she ordered, forcing every ounce of conviction she could manage into her voice .

"Damn you, Furlorian," the admiral snarled. "Stay your hand. I'll order my troops back. Don't do anything rash."

"It's not me who'll be doing it, Galforin, but you," she countered. "Call your people off now or I'll set Krawlas ablaze."

She glanced at Dent, and the AI placed his hand on the wall. Galforin gave the order and returned his glare to Taj. She heard the command relayed behind him.

After a few tense moments, Dent nodded and gave her a thumbs-up.

Taj growled at the admiral, "Don't do anything stupid like that again."

The AI cut the link, and Taj groaned, slumping to the floor.

"That was close," she mumbled, rubbing her temples.

"He'll find another way to get at us," Dent told her. "I can't monitor much of the area under the outpost. We got lucky finding this, Jak's guy leading us to it."

She nodded. "Speaking of Jak, I think it's time we had a talk with him."

He'd run off after learning of the Wyyvans tunneling their way and said nothing to Taj or her people, made no effort to warn them.

That didn't sit well with Taj.

She'd believed things were settled when she offered to give the rebels a way off the planet in exchange for their help one last time.

Apparently, she had been wrong.

She hoped they weren't doing something stupid that would compromise all their lives.

As bad as she felt about how things had worked out, she couldn't let that happen. There was too much at stake.

CHAPTER SIXTEEN

"I thought we had an agreement," Taj said to Jak once she found him and his people.

He stiffened at hearing her speak, and Rat's eyes narrowed as she looked at them.

"What does she mean, Jak?" Rat asked.

"Stay out of it, Rat," Malcolm warned. "This isn't your place."

"Not my place?" she shouted back. "Are you serious? How the hell is it not my place? I'm right here with you, aren't I?"

Jak raised a hand for her and Malcolm to stop arguing and met Taj's eyes.

"The Wyyvans are digging their way into the tunnels," he explained. "There's no more time to plot and plan. If we're going to get out of here, it has to be now. We can't wait."

"So even though we gave you a way out, you were just

gonna leave and not even tell us that the enemy was about to break down the walls?" Taj asked.

"*You* put us in the situation," Malcolm growled, "so don't expect us to get you out of it. Our loyalty is to our own."

Rat glared at him, still looking around. "Wait, you knew the Wyyvans were coming into the outpost and you didn't warn anyone?"

"Our people know, and we're getting out of here," Jak stated.

"You didn't tell *me*," Rat complained.

Malcolm shrugged. "Seems like you switched sides the moment that cat impressed you, girl. We'd have given you the chance to decide, but it wouldn't make any sense to say anything if you'd just run and tell them, now would it?"

Rat growled and shook her head. "Is this what we've become? Cowards who run away at the slightest threat?"

"This isn't some small threat, Rat," Jak told her. "The Wyyvan are going to crush us in here, storming the outpost from the inside *and* out."

"That's not the case," Taj explained. "We've warned them off."

"And we're just supposed to take your word for it?" Malcolm said, dragging the last out into a hiss.

"I'm not saying he's going to hold off forever, no, but we know why he hasn't just assaulted us from space," she answered. "We're sitting in a planet-sized bomb of Tora-dium-42."

Jak's eyes went wide as saucers.

"Even more reason for us to get out of here," Malcolm stated. "That just makes it easier for him to kill us."

"He's not willing to risk his stash," Taj reasoned. "That's why we're still here, and why he hasn't used his fleet to bombard us. If he blows the outpost, he loses the planet and all the Toradium-42 it has to offer."

"How's that keep him from storming us to take it back?" Jak asked.

"I...uh...threatened to detonate it," Taj admitted.

"You *what?*" Malcolm shrieked. "You're insane!"

"I don't actually plan to do it," she told him. "I just needed Galforin to believe I would in order to buy us more time."

"You're as dangerous as the lizards." Malcolm shook his head. "We'll take our chances running."

"You'd be a fool," Dent stated. "Outside the outpost, you are an easy target—one that doesn't require restraint by the Wyvvans. They can come at you with everything they have."

"They'll have to find us first," Malcolm countered. "Loose groups out in the open desert? They won't even know we're out there."

"Except that their fleet is within scanner range, and they still have fighters in the air, which have been circling the area since we took over the outpost. You *will* be found, and you *will* be killed, and there's nothing we can do to help you," Dent went on.

"You'd be making a mistake running now," Taj warned. "While we certainly can't guarantee your safety, we can give you a fighting chance and get you into a destroyer that you can use to defend yourselves."

"And all we have to do is put targets on our backs while

you formulate some wild plan that's supposed to save the day?" Malcolm challenged.

"How is that any different from what you're suggesting?" Rat asked. "Either way, we're risking our lives running. One way gives us a chance to get off-planet, while the other leaves us here hoping the Furlorians win," she argued. "Because if they don't, it'll just be a matter of time before the lizards come looking for us, to kill or enslave us again."

"We can get you and your people out of here, Jak," Taj reasoned, talking to Jak instead of the irrational Malcolm. Her best chance lay in convincing Jak that she and her crew were the best options for the rebels' safety. If they ran now, Taj wasn't sure she could save them or her people.

Their survival hinged on one another.

"So, you want us to sit on a bomb until you deem it's the right time to go?" Malcolm went on. "This is a mistake, Jak."

"Maybe," the rebel leader admitted.

Malcolm scoffed. "You aren't taking any of this seriously, are you?"

"We're in danger no matter what we do," Jak told him. "Having a destroyer at least puts us in a position where we get to determine our own fate. How long do you think we can realistically survive in the desert, Malcolm? Especially if the Wyyvans win?"

"As long as we need to," he spat.

"You're being unreasonable," Jak said. "We've survived this long because the lizards didn't give enough of a damn to keep track of our numbers. They didn't know we were out here, but now they do. There won't be any hiding and skulking in the tunnels anymore."

"So, we're just supposed to let these people dictate how we go out?" Malcolm shouted.

"It's not that simple," Jak argued.

"It really is, Jak," Malcolm shot back. He gestured to the Furlorians. "These are the people the lizards want, not us."

"What are you suggesting, Malcolm?" Rat asked, inching forward and sneering at him. "That we turn them over to the lizards and cut a deal?"

There was the barest of pauses before Malcolm answered, and Taj realized that if the opportunity presented itself, that was exactly what the male would do.

"I'm not saying that," he replied. "I'm simply stating that the lizards are focused on the cats right now. We're not who they want. They don't even give a damn about us," he explained. "If we make a break for it, the Wyyvans will focus on them, not us. We can get out of here."

"You keep missing the bigger picture, Malcolm," Rat argued.

"And that fact that you need a young girl to point it out makes me question your faculties," Dent added.

Malcolm snarled at the AI, "You just want us to play nice, so you can use us as bait so *you* can get away."

"I'm not going to lie," Taj told him, whiskers flicking with irritation, "we need your help to get out of this situation. We can't do what we need to do without sufficient bodies on those shuttles, but we're not hanging you out to be killed. We're taking a calculated risk that we can get you aboard a ship and get you out of here while accomplishing our own goals at the same time."

"*Bait*," Malcolm spat in response.

"We're all at risk," Taj countered. "Whether we like it or not, and regardless of whose fault it is, we're in this together now. If you run, you're gonna die. Then we die shortly after. It's as simple as that."

Dent stiffened, and Taj glanced at him with a questioning look. "What is it?"

"The Gate is powering up, and the Wyyvan fleet is advancing again," he reported. "They're bringing their troop carriers into play, positioning them to give them cover so they can reach the planet and defend the Gate at the same time."

It'd happened sooner than she'd expected, but she had known Galforin would be cowed for only a short time. Because of that, she needed to advance everything and hope it worked.

Taj tapped Dent on the arm and nodded, letting him know to move forward with what they'd planned.

"How convenient," Malcolm accused. "Of *course* they've chosen to push forward while you're pitching your idea. It helps you pressure us."

Dent raised his arm and activated his view screen, showing both Malcolm and Jak the view from the *Decimator*. The enemy fleet moved forward as the AI had reported.

"How do we know this is real?" Malcolm asked, unwilling to believe anything.

Taj groaned. There was no way she was going to convince the male that she had *all* of their best interests in mind, not just her own.

But the push of the Wyyvan fleet was actually a good

thing from a tactical point of view. She just needed to make the rebels understand that.

"Look, Jak," she started. "We have contingencies in place, one moving ahead right now, which *should* help turn the tide in our favor, or at least be a good distraction, but it's not gonna do any of us any good if we're sitting here arguing about all this. We need to be united, then once we're back in space, you and your people can do as you will and leave us behind if you want."

Malcolm shook his head. He wasn't budging.

Jak was another matter.

He stared at Taj, and she could see the faintest glimmer of hope and uncertainty in his eyes. He wanted to believe, wanted to trust her and let her help lead his people out of their enslavement, but Malcolm was a strong presence.

She suspected he'd been the one to get inside Jak's head earlier, convincing him not to let the crew know the Wyyvans were coming.

Taj pushed, hoping to sway Jak.

"Threatening to blow up the Toradium-42 cache was a bluff to buy time, that's all. I'm not homicidal *or* suicidal. I want us all to get out of here safe and sound," Taj explained. "We knew it wouldn't give us much, but Galforin flinched. That's given us an opportunity to get some of our assets into play. The admiral moving his pieces across the board only helps our cause. You have to believe that."

"I don't see how it can," Jak argued, still unsure. "They're going to land more troops on the planet. We don't stand a chance against the force that's already here, let alone one that's a hundred times its size."

"That's why we want you on those shuttles," she argued. "It helps us both, but we only have a few more minutes before the moment of truth is upon us. If we're not in place and ready to get your people out of here, all of our opportunities are gonna evaporate. We'll be stuck here, ready to be overwhelmed."

"I won't do it." Malcolm snarled. "This is a mistake, Jak. They're using us."

"Shut the hell up!" Rat shrieked, punching Malcolm in the chest and sending him stumbling backward. He toppled to a knee, staring up at the young female with wide, surprised eyes. "If you want to stay here and die, that's on you, but you don't get to decide for the rest of us. I'm in."

Rat glanced at the gathered rebels and received numerous nods and mumbled encouragements.

Jak scanned his people and gave in with a nod. "We'll do it," he said in a quiet voice. There was still uncertainty there, but he'd made the right choice.

"Then get your people to the tunnel leading to the shuttles," Taj told him, wasting no more time.

"You heard her, people!" Rat called. "Get to those damn shuttles. Now!"

A few of the rebels cast furtive glances at Malcolm, who was still on his knees, but no one hesitated. All of them ran in the direction of the tunnel that led out of the outpost and to the shuttles Taj had had Dent prepare.

Jak helped Malcolm to his feet, and the older male snarled at Rat. Taj stepped between the two and shook her head.

"Decision time, Malcolm," she told him. "In or out, but

we can't sit here waiting for you. If you're not on one of the shuttles when they need to leave, you're getting left behind."

"He'll be on it," Rat spoke for him.

She grabbed his arm and dragged him off. He glared at the girl, but he went without fighting her. Taj watched them leave to make sure he didn't do anything.

"You need to go too," Taj told Jak. "Your people will need you."

He nodded, although he still appeared reluctant.

They didn't have time to wait, though.

Taj and Dent started off and Jak found his motivation, joining them. As they made their way quickly toward the tunnel, the AI held up his screen so they could all see it.

Like before, it had a view from the *Decimator*, and they could all see the enemy fleet advancing. Then there were two streaks of silver that hurtled toward the troop carriers.

"There are the shuttles," Dent reported.

Although Taj knew what was coming, she found herself holding her breath in anticipation. A lot rode on all the pieces falling into place at the right time, and these were the first.

The shuttles shot forward, and it was clear that the Wyyvan fleet was prepared for them. Weapons fire shifted from the Furlorian armada to the shuttles without hesitation, bursts of energy streaking toward the craft.

To their credit, the shuttles were ready. The two ships pivoted and dodged, pulling off maneuvers that would have been impossible had there been living, breathing crew members aboard.

The shuttles spun in tight circles and made jarring

turns, racing toward the troop carriers with their explosive load of Toradium-42 that Dent had had the bots put in while the shuttles were grounded.

Given how prevalent the mineral was on Krawlas and how close beneath the surface, the bots had been able to create their own mini-mining operation out of sight of the enemy, digging up a large quantity of the material.

It'd been how they'd exploded the other shuttles earlier, and the bots had been working non-stop to load other shuttles as well, preparing for this exact moment.

"Get the shuttles up and moving," Taj told the AI. Dent nodded, sending the message to the automated vessels.

The Wyyvans lashed out with everything they had at the approaching shuttles, and despite Dent's frantic efforts to keep them from harm as he steered them toward their targets, the onslaught was simply too much.

The first of the shuttles exploded, a brilliant flare of whiteness blurring the screen for a moment. Then, as the flash retreated, Taj caught sight of the second shuttle being shot down.

Like the other, its load of Toradium-42 made the explosion much larger than one would expect of such a craft.

But the Wyyvans had gotten to them early.

Jak sighed when he realized the shuttles had failed to get to a distance where they were a threat to the enemy fleet.

The destroyed shuttles flared out and died, and the enemy fleet and its troop carriers remained unharmed.

Jak stumbled as if the weight of the shuttles' failure had fallen onto his shoulders, but Taj grabbed his arm and kept him moving.

"The real plan has yet to be revealed," Taj told him, grinning all the while.

Jak's eyes focused on the screen as the trio reached the end of the tunnel. The gathering of shuttles tasked to take the rebels to the fleet above had mostly begun to liftoff, only one still remaining firmly on the ground.

The view on the screen shifted, and Taj spied the other two shuttles she'd sent circling around the planet earlier.

The Furlorian armada opened up on the Wyyvan fleet with everything they had, adding to the distraction. Taj swallowed hard as she watched the two shuttles creep closer.

It wasn't until they were nearly in place that the sole destroyer protecting the temporary Gate realized they were there. The ship spun around, unleashing its full arsenal upon the shuttles.

Taj grinned when they did. "Shoot first, ask questions later."

The shuttles darted toward the Gate as they were gunned down.

But it was too late.

Packed to the absolute limit of their open space, the two shuttles carried far more Toradium-42 than any of the other shuttles had. As a result, even the destruction of the shuttles far from the Gate wouldn't stop them from carrying out their deadly mission.

The shuttles exploded, and there was a wash of energy that wiped the screen's signal out, a snowstorm of static obscuring their view. Dent shut off the screen, smiling.

"And there goes the Gate," Taj told Jak, grinning ferally all the while. "Any reinforcements Galforin calls now will need to travel from the Zendarin Gate, which means there won't be anyone arriving anytime soon."

Jak stood there frozen, staring at the pair with wide eyes. "I don't—"

"No time for explanations," Taj told him, nudging him toward the last of the shuttles. "You need to get out of here. Join your people. We'll see you soon."

Jak stumbled to the shuttle and was helped inside by Rat, who offered Taj and Dent a sly wink.

Seconds later, the hatch was closed and the shuttle lifted off, streaking toward orbit.

Taj turned to look at Dent. "You think those devices you and Lina made will do what they're supposed to?"

"I wouldn't trust them to fool anyone under perfect conditions with clear scanners or a sharp scanner operator," Dent said, "but none of those circumstances exist here. They should do what's expected of them."

"I hope so," Taj muttered.

A lot of her plans had relied on subterfuge and sleight of hand, offering distraction after distraction in order to accomplish something else. Since she'd done it so often, she had to wonder when the grand admiral would catch on and stop playing into it.

She wasn't looking forward to that moment. Outnumbered, outgunned, and unprepared, she didn't have any other advantages.

Luck was a great thing to have on your side, but it wasn't something you could count on.

Fortunately, though, it could be manipulated to a small degree.

Taj planned to do exactly that.

CHAPTER SEVENTEEN

"All ships are in position," XO Volg reported. "Troop carriers are cleared for approach."

"And the Gate?" Galforin asked.

"Open and ready to receive the next wave, sir."

"Excellent." Galforin rubbed his hands together, imagining himself strangling the arrogant Furlorian who'd stood up to him.

She'd caused them too much grief already, damaging his ship and opposing him in a way no one else ever had.

The creature was an enigma.

He couldn't be sure if she was serious about blowing the planet up, but he couldn't take the chance that she was. So far, the Furlorians had been impossible to predict, throwing feints at his forces and striking out in ways Galforin least expected.

The admiral had realized this was part of her operations strategy, but he believed he had her figured out now. The aliens had come here with far less firepower and people than it required to take the planet back, and Galforin would use that to his advantage.

He didn't think the Furlorians wanted to commit suicide, but he wouldn't take that chance, so he'd had his people in the tunnels under the outpost pull back and await his command.

Those outside continued to press forward slowly, and Galforin had been surprised to note that the artillery hadn't yet been turned upon them. He figured it was only a matter of time until it happened, but he'd keep pushing his soldiers forward regardless.

"Shuttles incoming!" XO Volg shouted. "There's Toradium-42 aboard."

Despite himself, Galforin felt his heart ramp up with apprehension.

He'd seen what these shuttles could do.

"Take them out now!" he ordered, jabbing a finger at the XO. "Do not let them get anywhere near."

Volg didn't bother to acknowledge the command. He went to work, ordering the Wyyvan crew to engage with everything they had, the order carried across the fleet.

The *Stormfront*'s view screen became a blur of energy blasts as the entire fleet put everything they had into taking out the shuttles before they came too close.

The troops had seen what had happened with the shuttles before, so they didn't need motivation to take these out.

Grim silence invaded the bridge of the *Stormfront*, and every crewmember there worked diligently to waylay the shuttle attacks.

Galforin felt flushed, adrenaline spiking as the shuttles

evaded the concentrated fire of his fleet for a few moments. The odds were in the Wyyvans' favor, though.

At last, the shuttles were struck down, both exploding with a viciousness that set Galforin's hands trembling.

These shuttles had been loaded with far more Toradium-42 than the last, and the explosions rattled the bridge of the *Stormfront* even from far away.

If that had struck us...

Galforin didn't finish the thought, unwilling to imagine how much harm the makeshift weapons might have caused had they gotten any closer.

"Do a sweep!" Galforin ordered. "I want to know if there are any more of those things headed our way."

"Oh..." Volg muttered a moment later. "Two more incoming."

"Take aim and fire!" Galforin screamed.

The XO gasped. "The fleet's not the target," he announced.

"What could possibly—?"

Then it struck him.

The Gate!

"No!" Galforin shouted, adjusting his view screen to get a better look at the approaching shuttles.

The destroyer he'd left behind to guard the Gate moved into position immediately and for an instant Galforin was proud of its captain, believing there was a chance they could stop the makeshift missiles from harming the Gate.

Then Volg's voice penetrated his ears.

"Scanner readings are off the chart, sir," he called out. "There's more Toradium-42 on these two shuttles than there was on even the last two."

The grand admiral nearly choked. "Have the captain block their way," he ordered, barely managing to get the words out. "Put the ship between them and the Gate, but don't let him fire on them!"

The words had barely left Galforin's mouth when he saw the flash of weapons fire erupt from the nose of the destroyer left to guard the Gate.

Galforin's stomach churned as the burst struck the first of the shuttles, which hadn't even tried to evade.

The resultant explosion blinded the *Stormfront* and rattled the ship to its frame.

Galforin sat there shocked, clawing at the armrests of his seat as the systems worked to adapt to the brilliance and clear the view screen. Moments later they succeeded, and Galforin cursed his sudden ability to see again.

He didn't like what he saw.

The Gate had been obliterated, leaving nothing but floating debris where it had hung in space moments before.

The destroyer nearest the Gate had fared little better. Pieces hurtled away from the blast point, tumbling into the darkness of space trailing debris, all that remained of the ship.

But that hadn't been the whole of the damage.

One of the troop carriers that had been near the rear of the fleet was engulfed. Its rear half had vanished, and the ship was venting atmosphere. It listed, rolling over slowly, out of control.

Two more nearby destroyers had suffered similar wounds. The first fell away, unable to right itself. The second limped along, but Galforin knew it had fought its last. It slowly drifted off as panicked calls for assistance rang out over the comm.

Galforin growled and cut communications, a weighty silence settling over the bridge.

He glared at the screen, disbelieving.

It wasn't until moments later when XO Volg caught his attention that he snapped to.

"Scanners are picking up ten shuttles coming from the planet," the XO reported.

Galforin hissed. "Where are they headed?"

"The enemy fleet," Volg said, clear relief in his voice. "One of the destroyers at the rear of the armada."

"Scan them!" Galforin shouted.

Volg looked at his console, examining the data. "I'm picking up traces of Toradium-42, but the shuttles appear to be loaded with lifeforms instead, although the signals I'm getting are distorted," he said.

"Distorted how?" the admiral asked.

Volg shrugged. "They're just unclear, sir, as if the electromagnetic surge of the explosions is impacting clarity. The lifeform readings are all over the place, too. I can't get a good lock on the signal to determine exact numbers."

"Are these the Furlorians?"

The XO shook his head. "Looks to me as if the shuttles are carting off our slave labor and token amounts of Toradium-42," he answered. "Scans of the outpost show that the Furlorians remain on the planet."

"Why would they do that?" the admiral asked.

It didn't make sense to him.

"Reading past the uncertainty of the scanner results, I'd

say the shuttles are full, Admiral," Volg answered. "My guess is that they didn't have enough room for everyone."

"Then now's the time, Volg," Galforin stated. "I want every soldier we have on the ground pushing into the compound and killing these rodents!"

"Yes, sir!" Volg replied, passing on the order.

While Galforin couldn't blow the Furlorians up from space just yet since the cache of Toradium-42 hidden under the outpost was too important, there was nothing the creatures could do to stop a full-scale assault while his soldiers emptied the chambers of the ore.

"And take out their damn fleet," he followed. "I want every one of those ships blown to dust."

The admiral grinned as Volg conveyed the order, adjusting his view screen so he could look down over the outpost and see what was about to happen.

The creatures would soon be dead, and he could return to his mining in peace.

CHAPTER EIGHTEEN

"Well, what do we do now?" Torbon asked. "The Wyyvans are advancing."

"We stand our ground for as long as necessary," Taj answered, "waiting for Dent to pull off the next phase of our plan."

"That hardly sounds enticing," Krawg muttered.

"Well, we've got the artillery units automated, so we can put them to use once the lizards get a little closer," she said. "And we've located as many of the Wyyvan tunnels as we could and set traps."

"Minor ones," Dent corrected.

Taj nodded. "Wouldn't be a good idea to set off big explosions down there currently."

"At least not until the Wyyvans finish emptying the storage chambers," Dent stated with a sly grin.

"The lizards are useful for *something*, at least," Torbon commented.

With the gear they'd brought down on the shuttles from

the armada, Dent and Lina had amplified his ability to be used as a seismic detector, giving them a better detection ratio for the tunnels the lizards had been digging.

The crew had known they were coming. It made sense that Galforin not only wanted his Toradium-42, but he'd also wanted the means to destroy the Furlorians wholesale. He could do that once the mineral was removed from the chambers beneath the outpost or the amount was reduced below a catastrophically explosive level.

The attack on them was simply to keep the Furlorians in place until that happened, Taj had realized that once Dent had detected the lizards breaking into the chamber even after she threatened to explode it all.

Galforin hadn't completely believed her, but he'd apparently been suspicious enough to tread carefully and back off for a bit.

That had been all Taj needed.

It gave them the opportunity to automate the artillery, enhance Dent's capabilities and, better still, take advantage of the confusion wrought by the massive explosions taking out the Gate to trick Galforin into believing the shuttles largely contained only people.

That was part of the plan Taj had been worried about. She figured Galforin would see through the ruse and concentrate his fire on the shuttles, but Dent reported that the transports had successfully docked on the destroyer they'd handed over to the rebels and the shuttles were now returning to the *Decimator* as arranged, their loads of Toradium-42 intact.

They were one step closer to retaking their home now.

Taj smiled at that thought, but there was still a lot to be done.

For now, they were trapped in the outpost on the planet, and the Wyyvan forces were pressing forward hard. It wouldn't be long before the fight started in earnest.

"The lizards are in range," Dent reported.

"Start hitting them with artillery fire then," Taj ordered, "but keep some of the units in reserve for those last fighters. We can't have them take out the guns too quickly or we're gacked."

Dent nodded, and the air was filled with the sound of cannon fire.

"Have the destroyers on the other side of the planet swing back around and get into range," Taj went on, ticking off an imaginary checklist in her head as she advanced each part of the plan in turn.

Unfortunately, there were factors she couldn't control, and those made her stomach churn. They'd been in several tight situations since they'd come back to Krawlas, but now she was counting on something that was completely out of her control.

She grunted and shook off the uncertainty that had grabbed her.

Taj was not sure of anything at the moment, except that she would fight to the end to free her planet from the grip of the lizards.

With the rebels aboard one of the destroyers, soon to be out of harm's way, she could concentrate on what she needed to do to reclaim her home world.

She glanced at the computer at her wrist, which was tied into Dent's jury-rigged seismic detector, and she caught sight of the blips that told her the Wyyvan soldiers were getting ready to breach.

"Set off the tunnel traps and seal those," Taj ordered Lina, who didn't hesitate.

A low rumble sounded, and the ground shook. Taj smiled as a large number of the blips flashed and disappeared seconds later.

Each blip represented one less Wyyvan who'd get the opportunity to gun them down.

"Is everyone in place?" Taj asked.

Cabe nodded. "They're where they should be. Jadie and Kal just reported their positions."

Taj retracted her helmet and told Cabe to do the same. As soon as he did, she leaned over and gave him a long, slow kiss. When she pulled away, she winked at him.

"I guess it's time for us to get into place too, huh?"

Her helmet reseated, and the crew moved down the labyrinth of tunnels that had recently been dug beneath the Wyyvan outpost. At this point, Taj was amazed that the place remained standing, with so much of its foundation dug away.

Fortunately, the tunnels had been dug deep enough to keep a relatively stable shelf of ground above their heads, but Taj worried it might come down on them before everything was said and done.

They ran to join the other Furlorians as planned, slipping through the tunnels and following a route that Dent had calculated would best avoid the influx of Wyyvan soldiers once they broke through their tunnels.

He'd been wrong.

Taj made her way around a sharp curve and stumbled

headlong into a squad of armored Wyyvans.

"Gack!" she cursed, raising her weapon and firing just as they did.

She blew away one of the lizards at close range, his chest smoking under his armor as he fell, but Taj had been hit too.

She grunted as several shots struck her, driving her back. She stumbled to her knees as the Wyyvans filled the tunnel with gunfire.

"Taj!" Cabe screamed, racing up behind her and unleashing a storm of fire on the lizards.

Krawg joined him a second later.

Dent grabbed Taj and yanked her out of the line of fire.

"Thanks," she muttered. Her ears rang, and her head swam inside her helmet. "That hurt."

Lina cast a concerned glance her way as she and Torbon leaned around the corner and picked their shots, firing past the others in the hall.

Taj shook her head and pulled free of Dent as the med systems in her suit kicked in. A warm, comforting feeling filled her veins, and she grinned at the sudden lack of pain.

"I love these suits," she mumbled, shaking off the lingering aftereffects of the injury.

She was going to hurt like gack for the next few days, but right now she felt fantastic.

She stepped farther into the tunnel and joined the fight again. A few heated moments later, the squad of Wyyvan soldiers was dead, scorched heaps lying on the ground.

But they'd served their purpose.

"We have more soldiers closing on us," Dent reported. "We're being cut off from Jadie and Kal and the others."

Taj cursed. "Can we circle around them?"

"Not without running into more," the AI told her.

"Then we go straight through," she decided. "Let's go."

"I liked you better when you were indecisive," Torbon said as they moved on.

"What?" she shot back. "I thought you liked the excitement?"

"Excitement, yes," he answered. "Running into gun and knife and spaceship fights in front of us, not so much."

"Well, at least you won't die bored," Cabe joked.

"I'd rather not die at all, which is kind of my point," Torbon countered. "Is there such a thing as boring excitement?"

Another group of Wyyvan soldiers stormed the tunnel before anyone could answer. Dent was struck by blaster fire twice and Lina once, but their armor deflected the majority of the damage.

Torbon leapt forward with a howl.

His blades now jutted from his forearms, and he whipped them in vicious side-to-side slashes. A Wyyvan helmet bounced away spewing black blood, the lizard's head still inside.

A second Wyyvan lost his gun hand and half his weapon. The pistol exploded, blowing the soldier back into his companions. He shrieked as he fell.

Then Torbon dropped low and pushed into the crowd of soldiers, hacking and slashing and stabbing, killing anything that got in his way.

The rest of the crew ran up behind him after checking on Lina, blowing away the last of the soldiers before Torbon could get to them.

He spun, his visor hiding the fury that twisted his expression. He saw Lina and his shoulders slumped. Torbon let out a relieved sigh.

Lina smiled and gave him a quick hug to let him know she was okay.

"You coming or what?" Jadie asked over the comm.

"We ran into a bit of interference," Taj told her.

"Need us to circle back?" Torbon's aunt asked.

"Stay put," she ordered. "We'll let you know if we run into trouble we can't handle."

"Roger that," Jadie came back, but Taj could tell the queen was debating whether to disobey and come after them.

Taj hoped she stayed put.

Too many lives were at risk already, and she didn't think she could handle it if the Furlorians who'd volunteered to join them on this mission ended up hurt or dead.

They'd lost too many to this war with the lizards.

"Let's keep moving," she urged, and they pressed on.

More and more lizards stumbled across them.

They fought on, making the most of their armor and weapons advantage, but the Wyyvans were relentless. No one among the crew escaped damage, and despite Dent's efforts to stay out in front and let his android body absorb more than the flesh and blood of his friends, the lizards were wearing them down in the tight confines of the tunnels.

After a harsh fight with ten of the lizards, who rushed forward with a zeal that bordered on bloodlust, Taj and the crew limped their way down the tunnel, favoring their wounds.

They were nearly there.

Dent groaned. "Two more destroyers have fallen," he reported, unwilling to meet Taj's eyes. He just kept marching, determined to make it out of the labyrinth under the outpost.

"How much longer?" Taj asked.

The AI grunted. "The ship is nearly ready."

"'Nearly' isn't exactly a precise measurement," Krawg muttered.

Two Wyyvans raced around the corner then, and Dent blasted the first and shouldered past the dying lizard to grab the second by his visor.

He twisted and drove the Wyyvan's head into the wall. The sharp crack of the soldier's helmet giving way echoed through the tunnel, and Dent followed that up by shooting the male in the head. Then he tossed the body.

"'Nearly' is as precise as I can manage right now," Dent went on.

The Ursite raised his hands in mock surrender after what he'd just witnessed. "I'm okay with that."

"Good," the AI mumbled, and it was clear that even *he* was feeling the pressure of the constant fight.

Although there was a copy of his Dandrinite memories, the entire sum of his people's knowledge and existence, back on Corzant, it was clear to Taj that he was beginning to think that they might not succeed here on Krawlas.

That meant that Dent might not be around to witness the rebirth of his people.

Taj felt for the AI. Although she was sure the Federation would find someplace where the Dandrinite society could be resurrected, she understood that Dent wanted to be the one to deliver them to that place.

Now, with the Wyyvan having managed to slip past the makeshift seismic monitor Dent had been using, uncertainty hung in the air.

"We need to get out of here," Taj said, more to herself than anyone else. The pressure was starting to get to her too.

Slower than she liked, they kept pushing forward, weapons out and hunkering down to fight every time the Wyyvans found them and attacked.

They had to have killed fifty of the lizards before they reached the cutoff that led to where Jadie and the others would be waiting.

Unfortunately, a good twenty Wyyvan soldiers stood there in the broad tunnel, guns out and ready.

"How many of these gacks do we need to kill?" Torbon whispered.

"All of them," Cabe replied.

"And then some," Dent added. "The soldiers above have gotten past the artillery units and are now inside the compound, dismantling the weapons and hunting us down."

"Hey, more good news," Torbon whined. "Got anymore?"

Lina groaned.

"As a matter of fact," Dent answered, "the Wyyvan fleet is pushing ours back. We've lost two more ships, and a third is on its way out. At least the destroyer with the rebels has moved out of orbit and is far enough away to have a legitimate chance of escape if things go wrong."

"*If* things go wrong?" Krawg asked.

"The fight's not over yet," Cabe assured.

"How much longer do we have?" Taj asked the AI.

"Minutes. Three, maybe four," Dent told her, but are you sure you want to do this still?"

"What choice do we have?" she countered. "We're not exactly spoiled for options."

"Well, not that I'm an expert or anything, but the idea of war is to take out your enemy, not yourself," Dent explained.

"You're not into the whole sacrifice thing, huh?" She laughed.

"I'm certainly not," Torbon told her.

"Well, for what it's worth, with all we've learned this time around, we'll be better prepared for the next war we get into," she offered.

"I'd be perfectly happy if we never fought another one, to be completely honest," Lina announced. "Not my thing, I'm realizing."

"It shouldn't be anyone's," Krawg stated.

"But here we are," Cabe said. "And we've got to get through these guys so we can meet up with Jadie and Kal and the others." He gestured to the Wyyvan soldiers who filled the tunnel.

"Lead the way," Torbon mumbled.

Since she'd been the one to get them all into this, Taj figured that was her job, not Cabe's. She sucked in a deep breath, readied her weapons, and bolted down the tunnel toward the soldiers, guns blazing.

It was as good a time as any to kick lizard ass.

CHAPTER NINETEEN

Taj blurred her form with the camo program to help sow confusion and raced toward the line of Wyyvan soldiers.

Unlike the previous narrow tunnels that had kept her restrained, unable to move around, the wider section here that led to the Toradium-42 chamber Galforin's soldiers had created gave her room to maneuver.

She feinted left, then darted right, strafing the lizards to keep them off-balance. They scrambled around, trying to avoid being shot, but that hadn't really been Taj's plan. She wanted to do this up close and personal.

The blades in her armor ejected as she hit the Wyyvans, tearing into them. The first lizard swallowed her weapon when she stabbed him in the face, the sharpened point easily slicing through his visor.

She whipped that blade free and swung it around, catching another lizard in the chest. A blackened line formed where she cut through his armor, and she left him to the others as he stumbled away.

Taj grinned as she went after another of the soldiers. He managed to get a shot off, but she ducked and the blast seared above her head, sparks illuminating the tunnel.

As much as she dreaded the consequences of battle, there was nothing quite like it, in her experience.

She lived for these moments.

All the plotting and planning was stressful and aggravating, and the waiting for things to happen, the action and reaction, left her worn out and drained, but the thrill of the fight was another thing entirely.

Taj rose to draw the aim of her opponents only to duck and dive at their legs as they took the bait and filled the tunnel with gunfire.

She rolled across the stone floor and stabbed one of the lizards in the gut. He bent over with a curse and Taj drove her helmeted forehead into his visor, shattering it. She saw his wide, panicked eyes for just an instant before she ripped her blade free and sent him tumbling away.

Cabe came up behind her and shot the lizard, killing him before he even hit the ground. As he had since the start, he clung to Taj's heels, fighting to make sure nothing happened to her.

She gave him a broad grin he couldn't see and kept on tearing into the lizards.

Krawg roared as he joined the fight. Using his size and strength, he flung lizards around as though they weighed nothing. Bodies flew, adding to the chaos.

A number of Wyyvans were gunned down by their own people since there was too much going on for them to accurately assess who was who in the crowded, blood-soaked corridor.

Krawg slammed one of the lizards to the ground with a howl. The snap of the soldier's neck was audible even through all the confusion.

But the hulking Ursite didn't stop there.

He grabbed the lizard by the ankles and lifted him into the air, swinging him like a club.

Armor clanged into armor as he used the dead Wyyvan as a weapon, smashing him into the others as he waded into their shattered ranks.

"Rowl!" Torbon shouted.

Not to be outdone by Krawg, Torbon had procured a second pistol and was moving down the hall alternating shots, cutting a swath through the lizards as if they were target dummies.

Target dummies that bled.

Taj was grateful for the filters that kept the realities of battle at a distance. Mostly the smells, but there was no mistaking what was going on there.

The Wyyvans' black blood coated the walls and floor and even the ceiling as the Furlorians pressed on, taking out one lizard after another.

Taj was slammed into the wall by a lizard she hadn't seen sneaking up behind her.

Strong hands wrapped around her and flung her to the side, and she collided with stone. Bright lights exploded in her eyes as her head struck the wall and she felt her legs go weak, threatening to buckle beneath her.

Weaponless, the lizard hissed in her face and pummeled her before she could catch her breath and clear her head.

He was relentless.

Blow after blow landed, and her armor's med system worked to overcome the pain and confusion, but deep down, Taj knew it was up to her.

She snarled at the lizard and drove a fist into his chest with all her might.

He gasped, and Taj felt his armor give way under her blow. The lizard stumbled back a step, and that was all the opportunity Taj needed.

She brought up her knee, driving it into his stomach and doubling the lizard over. Then she clasped both hands together and drove her fists into the back of the Wyyvan's head.

He crashed to the ground face-first, helmet bouncing off the stone floor, but she didn't stop there. She raised her boot and stomped over and over until the soldier stopped resisting and went limp.

Taj sighed and stumbled into the wall, panting.

"You okay?" Lina asked as she moved to her side.

Taj nodded.

"I'm good" she managed to answer, using the momentary excuse of her injuries to survey the scene.

The crew had decimated the ranks of the lizards, taking out more than half of them in just the few moments they'd been fighting.

Still, the effort was taking its toll.

Cabe fought on, as did Krawg, but Dent and Torbon had fallen back, shifting their focus to the narrow entryway that led to the Toradium-42 storage chamber.

Blocking the entrance to keep any more of the lizards from coming through or leaving, the pair had stopped driving into the enemy, and it had an immediate effect on the fight.

The lizards dug in and pressed forward. A pair charged at Taj as she stood there recovering, but Lina didn't hesitate.

She opened up with her rifle and sprayed the two lizards. They shrieked and stumbled, appearing to almost dance as the gunfire tore into them.

It wasn't until she eased off the trigger that the two could fall. And they did, dropping like sacks of stones to add to the body count on the ground.

Taj caught her breath and triggered her comm. "How much longer, Dent?"

He knocked a Wyyvan to the side and shot him in the ribs, backhanding him away before responding, "The ships are in motion now."

Taj couldn't help but smile.

The last of her plans were coming to fruition.

Although she'd had far too few when they'd returned to Krawlas, they'd adapted and overcome, using their circumstances and surroundings to their advantage. Now it was time for the culmination of all they'd worked for.

The moment of truth was upon them.

It was time to end this.

She mustered her strength, ignoring the stiffness and pain that nagged at her—those the med systems were unable to completely nullify—and pressed ahead.

"Take them out *now*!" she shouted, rejoining the fight.

Krawg and Torbon, off to the sides, let loose sprays of gunfire, taking out any of the lizards in their way.

Cabe and Dent pushed forward. The pair ripped

through the enemy, Cabe floating loosely behind the AI, moving from side to side and firing around Dent, who went straight at the enemy, a blade carving a path on one side as he gunned down soldiers on the other.

Lina stayed close to Taj, and the engineer sprayed the remaining lizards with automatic fire while Taj picked her shots and kept the enemy from getting in a good shot on any of her people.

A few moments later, the fight was over.

Smoke filled the tunnel, a hazy, drifting reminder of what had happened there.

"Get inside," Taj ordered the crew, motioning for them to slip into the Toradium-42 chamber.

This was the part of the plan Taj had been the most worried about.

She tossed small, makeshift explosive devices down the tunnel in each direction and took cover behind the wall of the chamber.

As well-conceived as the plan was, there was still the chance that explosives of any size would set off the cache of minerals she and the crew were sitting on.

If that happened, they wouldn't even know.

Regardless, Taj clenched her teeth and narrowed her eyes as the two devices exploded.

There were two loud whumps that melded into one another, and then a wave of dust and dirt washed past the entrance, blacking out the tunnel. Debris clattered just beyond the rough-hewn doorway, and stones and rubble clattered, tumbling and crashing together to seal off the hallway outside.

A few moments later, the rumbling stopped and the

tremors in the ground ceased.

Taj breathed a sigh of relief.

They were still there.

Lina slapped her on the shoulder in her excitement.

"We did it," she yelled.

Taj wanted to celebrate, but it wasn't over yet.

"Let's find Jadie and the others," she replied.

The pair joined the rest of the crew, and they made their way through the massive chamber of Toradium-42, boots sinking into the soft mineral.

The trip was surreal.

Dunes of the mineral sprawled before them as far as they could see. Taj had realized how much Toradium-42 there was on the planet, but seeing so much of it collected in one place was nearly overwhelming.

She could see nothing *but* the mineral, and despite knowing she was the safer there than she'd been anywhere since returning to Krawlas, a cold chill skittered down her spine.

There was simply too much power collected in that chamber to not be afraid of it.

Though the Wyyvan soldiers had worked to dig it out and move it, they'd barely made a dent before Jadie and Kal had ambushed them.

The Furlorians had crept through the same tunnels Taj and the others had, sneaking up on the soldiers as they worked to empty the chamber. And since the lizards had no clue that their enemy knew they were there, they had been caught totally off guard.

Jadie and Kal and the rest of the Furlorians had struck hard and fast, waiting until the lizards were all in the tunnels, returning from dropping off a load of the mineral and coming back for more.

Jadie, her helmet retracted, grinned as Taj and the crew made their way over to where they stood in front of the array of tunnels the lizards had dug into the chamber.

Wyyvan soldiers littered the ground just inside the tunnels, left where they'd died, curled up like dead insects in the dark.

Taj came over and hugged Jadie, returning the woman's grin. "You did good," she told her.

"It's easy when they don't know you're coming," she replied, chuckling. "Besides, Kal helped a little."

"A little?" Kal growled. His whiskers flittered.

Krawg patted him on the shoulder as he glanced down a tunnel to admire their handiwork. "Don't let it bother you," he told Kal. "It's their world. They just let us live in it."

Cabe laughed. "Ain't *that* the truth."

"Damn straight," Lina joked, grinning all the while. "And when this is all over, I expect a back rub and break-fast in bed."

Torbon sighed. "*Greeeeeat!* Shoot me now."

Taj grinned and came over to stand beside Krawg, looking down the tunnel. "Don't tempt me."

Before Taj could ask the question on her mind, Jadie answered it.

"These tunnels lead into the foothills surrounding Everon's Canyon. There's a gathering of vehicles there that the Wyyvans were using to transport the Toradium-42, but there was no way they were gonna get it all out of here. It would have taken weeks."

"I don't think Galforin thought that part through," Taj

replied. "I suspect it was more of a fallback plan should his troops not take us out."

"Well, he certainly didn't expect us to use his own tunnels against him." Jadie laughed.

"No, I can't imagine he did," Taj agreed. "And speaking of using the tunnels, I think it's time to get the gack out of here. The lizards will break through our blockade soon enough, and I don't know about any of you, but I'm too tired to play run and gun anymore."

The rest of the crew agreed, and they all slipped into the tunnels, making their way toward the surface of Krawlas.

As Taj walked, she wondered if she'd get to see the last of her plan play out.

As much as she dreaded what was going to happen, what they would lose, it was a fair trade if it worked out the way she hoped.

She resisted offering up a prayer to Rowl, knowing the finicky god would do as she pleased regardless, so what was the point?

If the Furlorians were meant to win, they would.

Taj would know in a few minutes if that were the case.

No matter what happened in the skies above, they'd given it their all.

No one could take that away from them.

CHAPTER TWENTY

Grand Admiral Galforin reveled in his success.

Reports of the battle came in sporadic bursts, and he couldn't help but grin as his troops broke past the hail of artillery fire and reclaimed the outpost. The guns, which had been automated by the enemy, had all been dismantled.

The last few fighters he had left had cleared the skies of opponents and circled looking for new targets, while the forces in the tunnels beneath the outposts continued to hunt down and engage the Furlorians at every turn.

He was winning, despite everything.

"Have we finished them yet?" Galforin asked.

Volg cleared his throat. "Not yet, but it won't be long. They've barricaded themselves in, bringing the roof down behind them. The soldiers are bringing the tunneling gear to bear and working to get in, our forces massing to make a concentrated push once they are through the debris."

"Excellent," the admiral crowed.

He'd lost so much since the arrival of the Furlorians, but it had been worth it to see them crushed.

The enemy armada had taken a beating at his hands, and although it continued to resist, the effort was taking a toll on it.

The Furlorians destroyers were falling away one by one, and their fleet was crumbling. There were barely enough ships to carry on the fight. Soon enough the command ship would be vulnerable, and Galforin would burn it to a husk and cast its remains into the cold depths of space like the cats had done to Captain Vort.

Everything was working out.

Galforin could picture himself returning to Belor Prime in victory, enough power at his fingertips to bring the Command Council to its knees before him.

No one could stand in his way.

Then, with all the might of the Toradium-42 available to him, he could take the fight to the Federation and tear their empire down around them.

He would be unstoppable, an emperor among peasants.

Galforin sank into his seat, unable to contain the grin that stretched his lips.

Soon, it would be all over, and he would rule, the true master of his destiny, no longer beholden to those fools on the Council.

He would show them...

"Uh...Admiral?" Volg's voice was a splash of cold water on Galforin's pleasant reverie.

"What is it, Volg?" he barked, anxious to return to his thoughts.

"Something's going on," his XO reported.

Galforin sat up, turning around to look at Volg. "What do you mean? Define 'something.'"

"The last of the Furlorian ships are massing, sir," he reported.

"Well, stop them," he ordered, clambering to his feet.

"We're trying," Volg replied, relaying orders to focus the fleet's fire on the gathering ships at the front of the enemy armada.

Galforin came over and examined Volg's screen so he could see exactly what the XO was seeing without exception.

The lull in weapons fire worried Galforin.

"Why aren't they firing at us, Volg?" he asked.

Volg examined his console before replying. "They're putting all their energy into their defenses, Admiral. Reinforcing their shields."

The Furlorian fleet adjusted from a spread-out mass of ships that had worked to evade the Wyyvans' fire to a mass of ships grouped together so closely that Galforin began to wonder where one ship ended and another began.

"What are they doing?" he asked, unsure what he was seeing.

Apparently, so was Volg.

"I...don't know, sir," he answered, shaking his head.

The enemy ships continued to gather, their shields linking and reinforcing each other. The gleam from their combined defenses was apparent, and the *Stormfront*'s scanners registered the interconnected web of shields as each ship added their power to the next.

It was as if they were forming...

"A wall," Galforin muttered, realization sinking in.

The admiral's heart skipped a beat.

"Why would they—" the XO started, but the reasoning became clear a moment later.

The command ship hung back, using the grouping of its destroyers as its shield. Seconds later, the entire mass accelerated and streaked toward the Wyyvan fleet, a massive battering ram of destroyers heading straight for them.

Galforin let out a choked gasp and grabbed his XO roughly by the shoulder. "Retreat!" he ordered without hesitation.

There was no doubt in his mind what the Furlorian fleet intended.

They were going to ram the *Stormfront*.

"Get us out of here, Volg," Galforin screamed.

The XO jumped to act, bringing the massive dreadnought around and peeling away from the rest of the Wyyvan ships.

"The fleet, sir?"

"Have them hold their position and take that wall of ships out," the admiral ordered. "I want them between it and us."

Volg grunted and complied, passing along the order.

Galforin didn't care if it chafed his XO to comply. The admiral refused to be taken out like some grunt, run down by an enemy fleet intent upon committing suicide to claim a victory.

The *Stormfront* accelerated, slowly beginning its efforts to evade the wall of ships coming its way.

That was when they started taking fire.

Shields flashed as two more of the enemy destroyers

appeared as if out of nowhere, having circled around the planet to sneak up behind the Wyyvan dreadnought.

Galforin growled. "Take them out!"

Volg loosed a volley of shots at the incoming destroyers, bursts of energy fire crashing into the enemy shields. The ships kept coming, as did those at their backs.

"Collision!" Volg shouted as the first of the enemy fleet crashed into the Wyyvan destroyers.

Focused on the enemy ships ahead of them, Galforin only saw the scanner view as several dots that represented his ships flashed and disappeared alongside several of the enemy's.

"They're not stopping," Volg reported, his voice cracking.

The two troop carriers were next to fall.

Slower than the other ships, less maneuverable, they struggled to put up a defense, but the effort was futile. The ships went up in flames that died as quickly as they erupted, the shielded destroyers of the enemy driving straight through them.

Galforin hissed.

Although he didn't give a damn about the lives lost, the ships represented years of hard work that he'd hidden from Command, his own personal fleet having grown and prospered under his command.

Now it was falling to ruin.

Worse still, there was nothing he could do about it.

"Get us out of here!" he ordered, knowing the XO's bark of confirmation was little more than lip service.

The enemy destroyers came at them, firing all guns. The *Stormfront* held its own, giving far better than it was getting, but that mattered little in the grand scheme of things.

As one of the destroyers flared and lost its shield, it veered off and swung about, streaking straight toward the *Stormfront*.

Its companion pushed harder, providing it cover.

"Watch out!" Galforin shrieked, but he knew there was nothing that could be done.

Slow as they were moving, the *Stormfront* having yet to gather speed, the collision was inevitable.

Although the ship was shredded by the dreadnought's guns as it approached, there was no stopping it.

It crashed into the side of the *Stormfront*, two goliaths colliding.

Alarms blared, the bridge bathed in crimson, and Galforin struggled to remain in his seat as the *Stormfront* shuddered at the impact.

Its shields deflected the brunt of the blow, but nothing could stop the momentum of the enemy destroyer.

As it broke apart across the hull of the *Stormfront*, dozens of systems failed in the dreadnought. Screens flickered, and flashing electrical shorts danced across the consoles as though lightning was gracing the night sky.

Fire suppression systems kicked in, and Galforin laughed at their ineffectiveness. What good was dousing spot fires when the whole ship was becoming an inferno?

Damage reports flooded in and Galforin ignored them. He didn't care.

He knew what was coming next.

He shifted the view to the wall of enemy ships and glared at it.

Although the Furlorians were losing ship after ship to the last of his fleet, they had done their duty admirably.

The enemy's command ship gathered speed and shot toward the *Stormfront*, streaking past the remaining Furlorian ships.

Loyal to the end, fools that they were, the Wyyvans focused their fire on the command ship but, undamaged by previous battles, it resisted all efforts, a deadly missile screaming straight toward Galforin.

As it drew closer, alarms screaming in his ears about the imminent impact, Galforin glanced at XO Volg.

"Let me guess...it's loaded with Toradium-42?" the admiral asked.

Volg didn't manage to reply, but Galforin knew the answer.

An instant later, the enemy command ship exploded, wiping out both fleets in a flare of destructive energy.

His last words were a curse that died on his tongue as he was incinerated.

CHAPTER TWENTY-ONE

The crew had scrambled from the tunnels into the open air.

Although they still had their helmets on, Taj believed it was the best-tasting air she'd ever breathed.

She was glad to be back on the surface after the crazy battles underneath.

It had been nonstop since they'd Gated in, and although the battle wasn't over, it was coming to a close one way or another.

Wyyvan bodies littered the ground where they emerged and Jadie scanned the area, admiring her handiwork.

"Now we just need to get out of here before the fighters pick us up and decide they want to play," Kal stated, staring at the sky.

"I don't think that's gonna be a problem much longer," Taj told him.

She stared at the outpost from the slightly raised vantage point of the hills. Wyyvan soldiers were a blur of motion beyond the wrecked walls, going house to house in search of anyone left behind.

"Good luck with that," Taj muttered under her breath.

There was no one left but Wyyvans and, soon there would be far fewer of those.

Dent had been quietly monitoring the situation in space, but he turned then, a wily grin stretching his lips.

"Contact," he announced. "The destroyers have reached the *Stormfront*."

A chill of exhilaration set Taj's fur on end, and she broke into a childish smile that colored her cheeks.

Dent raised his wrist screen above the crew so everyone could watch. The Furlorians crowded around, watching as the *Decimator* bore down on the Wyyvan command ship.

Taj cringed every time one of the Furlorian ships was destroyed, the makeshift wall they'd crafted falling apart brick by brick, but there was an underlying excitement that grew with every passing second.

One of the destroyers collided with *Stormfront*, crippling it, and the Furlorians cried out, cheering and clapping.

They all knew Galforin was on that ship, the slimy lizard who had forced them from their home and had sent them fleeing into space.

To see his ship listing and venting its atmosphere into space was one of the most satisfying moments Taj had ever experienced.

That was eclipsed by the arrival of the *Decimator*.

It broke through the lines, taking fire as it streaked toward Galforin's ship.

It looked like a giant missile as it closed on its target.

Taj held her breath, waiting for the collision she realistically knew didn't need to happen.

With all the Toradium-42 the shuttles had carted aboard, there was no stopping the *Decimator*'s deadly flight, regardless of what happened.

It was Death coming to settle the score.

Still, she couldn't bring herself to relax until she saw Dent trigger the ship's self-destruct sequence.

Taj looked away as the ship exploded, more because of its destruction than the brilliant flash that whited out the view screen.

It had been her order that had laid waste to the powerful ship the Federation had so generously given her, and she felt a pang of regret at its passing.

Up above, the explosion flared like a dying star, lighting the night sky and chasing away the darkness for a moment.

No need for the view screen. Taj stared up at the blast and marveled at its size and ferocity.

She kept waiting for the sound, despite knowing she would never hear it.

"Whoa!" Torbon muttered as the newly-born star expired and faded, night washing back over them.

It's almost over, Taj thought.

The flurry of Wyyvan movement lapsed into a coma.

All across the outpost, the soldiers stopped and stared at the sky as one. The remaining fighters streaked toward space, abandoning the planet and leaving streaks of shame in their wake.

Dent examined his computer again and nodded. "Both fleets have been annihilated," he reported.

Once more, a pang of regret tied a knot in Taj's stomach, but it was a fair price for what they'd gained, she thought.

"Well, we're only outnumbered a hundred to one now," Krawg mentioned, staring at the outpost and counting the enemy who remained.

"Easy work for a brute like you," Torbon told him.

The Ursite shrugged. "If I were so inclined. You can go first."

"Someone's gonna have to take them out eventually," Lina stated. "It's not like we have any ships to come in and clean them up anymore."

"Just the one," Dent replied.

The crew turned to look at the AI with questioning eyes.

He chuckled. "You didn't actually think Rat would let them leave, did you?"

Taj grinned. She hadn't expected the rebels to stick around, especially after they'd been forced to ride up to the ship on loads of the explosive Toradium-42.

"There aren't any shuttles left, however," the AI went on, "so it's not all good news. We have no way up to them."

"Could be worse," Cabe said.

Everyone agreed.

A flutter of movement at the outpost caught Taj's eye. The groups of Wyyvan soldiers began to fracture and they scattered through the compound, their organization failing as they learned that their entire command structure had been wiped out.

"Too bad the Wyyvans didn't get more of the Toradium-42 out before we killed them all," Kal said, looking at the tunnel entrance wistfully.

"We'll probably have to do it ourselves at some point," Taj said. "At least, after we clear the lizards out. We don't need them setting it off as a last resort."

"I don't think they understand how powerful the stuff is," Lina suggested. "If they did, they wouldn't have sat atop it so willingly."

"They've never been known for their wits," Krawg stated. "Except S'thlor. He's pretty smart for a lizard."

"The same way you're pretty smart for a walking rug," Torbon joked.

"Says the cat who walks on two legs," the Ursite shot back. "You'll have to show me your litter box one day."

While the crew bantered back and forth, the stress of their battles sloughing away, Dent turned to Taj.

There was still more work to do.

"How do you want to clean out the remaining Wyyvans?" he asked. "We can have the rebel destroyer threaten them and see if we can get the soldiers out into the open," the AI suggested. "That would be better than trying to go in with our small group and root them out one by one. Someone's bound to get hurt if we go that route."

As morning crept over the Maladorian Plains, shimmers of red and pink coloring the distant sky, Taj cast a glance over her shoulder at the canyon that sprawled behind her.

She retracted her helmet and breathed in the early morning air, holding it in her lungs for as long as she could before letting it out in a slow whistle.

Although it was hard to tell with all the destruction the

Wyyvans' mining operation had wrought across the scrub-land, Taj could taste the barest hint of moisture in the air, as well as the tang of blooming plants.

The hint of the season was evident in the steep mountains that made up Everon's Canyon, their russet colors shifting to a pleasant green. Taj could hear distant howls carried on the slight breeze that caressed her cheeks and set her whiskers fluttering.

"I have a better idea," she told him.

"Does it involve explosions?" the AI asked.

Taj shook her head. "Nope, but that doesn't mean it won't be fun."

"When you put it that way, I hate it already," Dent told her, grinning.

"What better way to get rid of an infestation of vermin than to let Nature take care of it?" she asked.

She turned and waved to the rest of the crew, motioning for them to follow her.

"Let's take a walk," she suggested. "I think we'll find exactly what we're looking for a few valleys over."

CHAPTER TWENTY-TWO

Taj whooped and hollered, firing her modified pistol into the air.

It had been three days since the crew had climbed out of the tunnels and made their way through Everon's Canyon, but now they were back.

And they weren't alone.

A herd of trrilacs accompanied them.

Great bulbous bodies flew gracelessly through the air, shifting with every coordinated flap of the multitude of colossal, membranous wings that extended from their spines and jutted out behind them.

Wide, round eyes shone like sparkling stars, staring into the distance above great gaping mouths. Millions of serrated teeth filled their maws.

It was in the trrilacs' nature to devour anything in their path.

While the "anything" used to be Culvert City and the balboran pens, that was no longer the case.

Now, the Wyyvan outpost and a mass of lizards who had yet to see the yearly migration of the great beasts stood directly in their path.

Taj and her crew used to ride the *Thorn* out every year —Cabe's precious windrider, long since destroyed in their first encounter with the Wyyvans—and steer the trrilac away from town and the herd of balborans.

Today, their job was different.

It was to make sure the creatures went straight at the outpost without veering off.

The crew ran at the far edges of the herd, firing stun bolts into the air to keep the creatures moving in the right direction.

The effort seemed wrong to Taj, in defiance of what she'd done since she was a kitten, but there was something satisfying about doing it.

The trrilacs had long been a difficulty the Furlorians had to surmount every year, the stubborn old Grans unwilling to move Culvert City out of the path of the creatures.

They'd believed it built character to have a regular challenge to surmount.

Taj thought that was stupid, but who was she to argue?

Now, the curse that had haunted them every year during the spring was now a blessing.

As the herd cleared the end of Everon's Canyon, something they hadn't done in over fifty years, they gathered speed. Giant wings strained to carry their weight, which was a big part of their threat.

The creatures would eat everything in their way, feeding in a frenzy and storing their food in their bellies for the continued trip northward. For the first few days, however, the trrilacs were too bloated to fly.

They would drop down on the city and balboran pens and chase every source of food they found, gorging until they could barely move.

That left a horde of giant carnivorous beasts that weighed tons.

They nestled in the wreckage of homes and barns and defecated everywhere, squirming in their filth and spreading it around until they regained the energy to fly again.

Then the whole herd would fly on, moving across the desert and disappearing until the next year.

"Oh, this is gonna be one gack of a wakeup call." Torbon laughed as he ran alongside Taj. "I hope there are ferion spider sacks all over these guys."

"Me too," Taj said, unable to stop grinning as they pushed the herd onward, shooting muted bursts of energy at their backs.

"Sucks that we'll have to clean up the mess these things make," Cabe said, "but I think it'll be worth it."

The crew slowing, having accomplished their mission. Taj went over to Cabe, wrapped her arm around him, and pulled him close.

It was the first time since they returned to Krawlas that they'd had a moment to melt into each other's arms. She rested her head on his shoulder as they trailed the trrilac herd, anticipation building.

The Wyyvans had settled into the outpost much like they had before, but with no mining going on, they had taken to scavenging.

After the total loss of contact with their commanders, the lizards were on their own, and they'd been on the planet long enough to know how harsh it was.

Like the rebels out in the desert, they knew there was a long, slow death awaiting them once they ran out of food.

At least it would have been had the trrilacs not swept through.

Alarms erupted in the morning air just before the creatures reached the outpost.

That was when the lizards regretted following their admiral's command of disabling the artillery units so they couldn't be used against the Wyyvan forces again.

Now they couldn't be used against *anything*.

Unable to hear the screams from a distance, Taj stood stoically and watched through her advanced optics as the trrilacs crashed down heavily across the compound, crushing anything and everything in their way.

Dozens of the giant creatures circled above, swooping down in thunderous arcs to pluck Wyyvan snacks from the ground. Taj was glad she couldn't hear the crunch of their armor as they were devoured, but there was no hiding the black blood that coated the trrilacs' lips and sharp teeth.

"We'll have to comb the tunnels under the compound to make sure we get all the lizards the trrilacs don't eat, you know?" Cabe said.

Taj nodded.

She suspected that task would be much easier once the herd of trrilac had finished their feast and moved on.

With all that weight atop the already uncertain shelf of ground, she figured there'd be a number of holes before the crew got there to clean them out.

Realistically, they could simply empty the Toradium-42 chamber that Galforin's soldiers had started, then have Jak and Rat blast the tunnels to dust and avoid going hunting altogether.

Either way, they had time now.

Taj chuckled at that.

They'd been under the gun since they'd arrived, and now they had all the time in the world to finish chasing the Wyyvans from their planet and rebuild.

In a few short days, Krawlas would be theirs again.

Memories of Gran Beaux and Mama Merr struck her, and she smiled.

No matter what losses the Furlorians had sustained, Taj knew the couple would be proud of her and proud of their people.

They had come home at last.

CHAPTER TWENTY-THREE

L ife was different on the new Krawlas.

It had been two years since the Furlorians had come back to their home world and stolen it back from the Wyyvan invaders.

None of the original settlers would recognize it now.

Where Culvert City had been was an open expanse of desert, a line of yellow tubes cutting across it and running all the way back to the eastern side of Everon's Canyon. The tubes were Lina's invention; a system of spark-cannons that could be triggered remotely that would guide the annual herd of trrilac away from settled land without anyone having to risk their lives to chase them away.

Taj missed that part of living on Krawlas, but that was really the only part.

The rest of the changes made life so much better.

Dent had resurrected a hundred of the Dandrinite's best and brightest using the information and techniques he'd kept secret ever since their extinction.

They embraced the idea of living alongside the heroic Furlorians and immediately started creating a better world for all of them.

It incorporated aspects of the old, rustic Krawlas that the Furlorians had grown up in, but there was a modernization to almost everything that amazed Taj even after all she'd seen in her travels.

With functional Gate technology and nearly endless resources, the Dandrinites were limited only by their imaginations—and sometimes not even that.

A sprawling metropolis of gleaming silver stood alongside the sleepy single-story town that was the new Culvert City, the two species co-existing without strife.

"I still can't believe how quickly they built all this," Taj marveled as she stared at the towering skyscrapers a short distance away from her porch.

Dent had made sure that none of them cast their shadows on the new Furlorian town.

She sat in the sun, baking under its heat and sniffing the air.

There were new scents since the Dandrinites had joined them, but they complimented the dry, dusty desert climate.

She could see the glimmer of a new lake that had been created in the Maladorian Plains, sunlight reflecting like diamonds off the surface.

"I can't believe I'm here to see it all," Rat remarked, her chair creaking as she eased it back. "I figured for sure that Jak and Malcolm would cart us off and we'd never set foot on this planet again."

"You people spent a long time here, slaving and

working the land," Cabe replied from his chair alongside Taj's. "That makes it your home, too."

Rat smiled.

Once Dent had released the rebel destroyer from his control, ensuring it was far enough away to avoid being damaged by the *Decimator*'s explosion, Jak had ordered the ship to return to the planet.

He and his people assisted in the cleanup after the trrilac herd had swept through, destroying the outpost and killing almost all of the lizards in their path.

They captured the remaining Wyyvans and had given them a choice.

To a lizard, they had chosen to surrender rather than face extermination. Taj had held them hostage for a short while, treating them far more kindly than their own commanders had. They were given an ultimatum when S'thlor arrived.

The blind Wyyvan had taken those willing to stay and be productive members of society under his wing.

Those who were less obliged were packed into shuttles and launched in the direction of Belor Prime with enough fuel and supplies to get there and a dire warning to never return.

The Furlorians on Corzant had come back with S'thlor, a message relayed to the Federation and the station by the rebels in the one remaining destroyer.

That was also something that had changed.

Culvert City bustled with activity, Furlorians flitting back and forth, Dandrinites and Wyyvan among them, along with the various races that had made up the rebels. Taj was at peace.

One of the first things the Dandrinites did when they awakened was protect the planet from hostile forces.

A great barrier encircled Krawlas now, advanced warships floating in orbit to reinforce it should it be necessary.

So far, it hadn't been tested, and Taj was grateful for that.

"You think they'll ever come back for the Toradium-42 again?" Rat asked.

"Let them," Cabe answered, chuckling. "I'd like to see them get past the Dandi shields and weapons systems. Besides, now that we've offered the Toradium-42 to the Federation, I'd like to see them try. I can't see General Reynolds letting them off as lightly as we did."

"I hope they don't," Taj mused, staring at the sky.

She'd had enough violence and bloodshed to last her a lifetime.

A couple of lifetimes, as a matter of fact.

She patted her swollen belly and smiled at the sudden flutter of movement inside.

Taj eased back in her chair, thinking about her past and her future. She remembered wanting all the excitement of traveling through space and battling strange, evil aliens once upon a time.

But that wasn't who she was now.

She had dreams of being like Mama Merr these days. She could rule from home, help raise her people, teach them how to be honorable, and let her children grow up to have the adventures and travel the universe.

This was their world now.

She had done her part to bring peace to it, and as long

as that reigned, she would be content to sit back and watch her children grow and prosper.

But Rowl forbid anyone ever dared to harm them.

She kept her armor and weapons in a case beneath her bed, and Taj would rise up in a heartbeat to defend her people and kids.

She might not have been born a warrior, but she'd become one over the last few years.

Both she and her crew both.

And should anything ever threaten their world, there'd be no more running. No, Taj, Cabe, Lina, Torbon, Krawg, Dent, and all the rest would suit up and take the fight to it.

No force in the universe could stop the crew if they were determined to do something.

And if the Federation ever needed them…they'd be there!

Besides, she still owed General Reynolds a pair of lizard-skin boots.

FINIS

AUTHOR NOTES - TIM MARQUITZ

JANUARY 4, 2019

Hey Folks! I appreciate you hanging out and reading this last book (and all the others, of course), and it's weird knowing we've come to the end here. At least of the current Furlorian saga. Thanks for sticking around and watching the cats battle their way toward better lives.

There was some discussion that they'd hadn't grown as much as some people believed they should have, but I'd always had it in mind that Taj and the others were always meant to be true to themselves. Taj wears her emotions on her sleeve, and this story arc was as much about the cats defying the odds as it was about remaining true to the nature of the characters, however flawed they might be.

While they would do what needed to be done, they were never going to be hardened warriors. They're cats! Independent, stubborn, and proud, they were always going to do it their way, for better or worse.

I appreciate the opportunity I've been given to share their story. I couldn't do this without the great folks at

LMBPN, Craig, Michael, Steve, Lynne, and the JIT team. Most importantly, I couldn't do it without you, dear readers. You're what makes this journey possible, and I'm forever grateful.

While we might have come to the end of the Enemy of My Enemy saga, I suspect you haven't seen the end of the cats, or of me, so I hope to see y'all around soon. Thank you so much for your support.

Tim

Thank you for reading! Once again, all the way to the end and beyond! I'm glad you liked this latest iteration of Enemy of My Enemy. Michael is not a cat guy, but he wants to be. He wants to retire to Cabo San Lucas where he can surround himself with the world's greatest hunters. Maybe not, but he's not opposed to cats, as long as they aren't climbing on him, unless they are.

It's not yet Christmas, but I have a heavy travel schedule over the next three weeks and don't want to forget these. Steve can be merciless in his kind reminders that the book is missing author notes and a blurb. At least we have a great cover by Tom Edwards already finished with typography by Jeff Brown. Together, they combine to make something that looks great. I hope it activates your imagination and juices your soul. There's such a great story in here. I hope you liked it.

Cat people! When Tim and I talked about this series over a year ago, I liked the idea of cats. They wreak havoc on our homes on the best of days and on the worst, Tasmanian Devil levels of destruction!

I don't have cats anymore. Turns out I was allergic, but I shall always remember those that graced my life for about 30 years. Lots of examples to choose from. If you have something on the edge of a table or desk, odds are better than 50/50 that they'll knock it off. If you try to stop them, odds increase to nearly 100%.

War is hell and costly, but when there's something worth fighting for, we love seeing the heroes emerge. They will put themselves in harm's way for their fellows. It's how heroes are made. There is no other choice for them. The logic is irrefutable.

Tim is a great co-author! Although this series is wrapping up, Superdreadnought will continue and who knows, we may see something new from the fertile imagination of Tim Marquitz.

If I were Michael, I'd be sitting here enjoying a Coke and checking how the plan to take over the publishing world is coming along. Probably pretty good, judging by the breadth and depth of great publications that are already available as well as what is coming.

Thank you for staying on board. It is a great ride.

Peace, fellow humans
Craig Martelle

BOOKS BY TIM MARQUITZ

Also Available from Tim Marquitz

The Demon Squad Series

From Hell (Novella)
DS1 - Armageddon Bound
DS2 - Resurrection
Betrayal (Intro short to At the Gates)
DS3 - At the Gates
DS4 - Echoes of the Past
DS5 - Beyond the Veil
DS6 - The Best of Enemies
DS7 - Exit Wounds
DS8 - Collateral Damage
DS9 – Aftermath
DS10 – Institutionalized
To Hell and Back - A Demon Squad Collection (books 1-3)

BOOKS BY TIM MARQUITZ

The Blood War Trilogy

Dawn of War
Embers of an Age
Requiem

Clandestine Daze Series

Eyes Deep (novella)
Influx

Standalone Fantasy

Dirge
Witch Bane
War God Rising

Sci-fi

Excalibur

Dead West

Those Poor, Poor Bastards
The Ten Thousand Things
Omnibus 1

Horror

Prey
Serial

Skulls
Heir to the Blood Throne: Inheritance

Collections

Tales of Magic and Misery

Non-Fiction

Memoirs of a Machine – w/John MACHINE Lober
Grunt Style: The Blue Collar Guide to Writing Genre
Fiction

Anthologies

Blackguards (Ragnarok Publications)
Unbound (Grim Oak Press)
SNAFU: Survival of the Fittest (Cohesion Press)
SNAFU: Hunters (Cohesion Press)
SNAFU: Future Warfare (Cohesion Press)
SNAFU: Black Ops (Cohesion Press)
In the Shadow of the Towers (Night Shade)
Neverland's Library (Ragnarok Publications)
At Hell's Gates 1&3 (Charity)
American Nightmare (Kraken Press)
Corrupts Absolutely? (Ragnarok Publications)
Widowmakers (Charity)
That Hoodoo Voodoo, That You Do (Ragnarok
Publications)

BOOKS BY MICHAEL ANDERLE

For a complete list of books by Michael Anderle, please visit:

www.lmbpn.com/ma-books/

All LMBPN Audiobooks are Available at Audible.com and iTunes

To see all LMBPN audiobooks, including those written by
Michael Anderle please visit:

www.lmbpn.com/audible

BOOKS BY CRAIG MARTELLE

Craig Martelle's other books (listed by series)

Terry Henry Walton Chronicles (co-written with Michael Anderle) – a post-apocalyptic paranormal adventure

Gateway to the Universe (co-written with Justin Sloan & Michael Anderle) – this book transitions the characters from the Terry Henry Walton Chronicles to The Bad Company

The Bad Company (co-written with Michael Anderle) – a military science fiction space opera

End Times Alaska (also available in audio) – a Permuted Press publication – a post-apocalyptic survivalist adventure

The Free Trader – a Young Adult Science Fiction Action Adventure

Cygnus Space Opera – A Young Adult Space Opera (set in the Free Trader universe)

Darklanding (co-written with Scott Moon) – a Space Western

Rick Banik – Spy & Terrorism Action Adventure

Become a Successful Indie Author – a non-fiction work

CONNECT WITH THE AUTHORS

About Tim Marquitz

Tim Marquitz is the author of the Demon Squad series, the Blood War Trilogy, co-author of the Dead West series, as well as several standalone books, and numerous anthology appearances. Tim also collaborated on Memoirs of a MACHINE, the story of MMA pioneer John Machine Lober.

Website: www.tmarquitz.com

Follow Tim on Facebook and Twitter.

Subscribe to Tim's newsletter and get up to date information on new releases as well as an Excalibur prequel story (exciting sci-fi) and Dawn of War, the first novel in the Blood War Trilogy (Epic Fantasy)!

http://www.tmarquitz.com/contact

Michael Anderle Social

Website: http://kurtherianbooks.com/

Email List: http://kurtherianbooks.com/email-list/
Facebook:
https://www.facebook.com/TheKurtherianGambitBoo
ks/

Craig Martelle Social

Website & Newsletter:
http://www.craigmartelle.com

Facebook:
https://www.facebook.com/AuthorCraigMartelle/

www.ingramcontent.com/pod-product-compliance
Lightning Source LLC
Chambersburg PA
CBHW050307110726
47899CB00007B/2143